THE HEALER

Aharon Appelfeld

THE HEALER

Translated from the Hebrew
by Jeffrey M. Green

GROVE PRESS
NEW YORK

Grove Press
841 Broadway
New York, NY 10003-4793

Published in Canada by General Publishing Company, Ltd.

LIBRARY OF CONGRESS CATALOGING-IN-PUBLICATION DATA
Appelfeld, Aharon.
[Be-' et uve-' onah ahat. English]
The healer / Aharon Appelfeld : translated from the Hebrew by
Jeffrey M. Green. — 1st ed.
p.   cm.
Translation of : Be-' et uve-' onah ahat.
I. Title.
PJ5054.A755B3813   1990
892.4'36—dc20   89-25847
CIP

ISBN 0-8021-3357-6 (pbk.)

Manufactured in the United States of America

Designed by Helen Barrow

First Edition 1990

3   5   7   9   10   8   6   4   2

THE HEALER

I

IN THE AUTUMN they arrived. The way had been long, exhausting, and toward the end it had been beyond the mother's strength. For two days they climbed the peak, exposed to wind and cold. Autumn is not a favorable season for journeys in these parts, but theirs was not a pleasure trip. Necessity, or whatever you wish to call it, had prodded them, and so they had set out. The father got off first: with a gesture of suppressed rage, he opened the door. The mother placed her foot cautiously on the earth and was immediately greeted with a furious glance, thundering with held breath, which said, "I told you, I told you a thousand times, but you wouldn't listen to me." The son and the daughter stepped down behind her in silence.

"Where might the inn be?" the mother asked in her old domestic manner.

"Don't ask me!" said the father without taking his eyes off her. She wanted to answer, "I wasn't asking you, I was asking the driver," but she restrained herself. The father shook his legs as though snow clung to his clothes. That was one of his most common expressions of anger.

"My dear," she turned to the driver, "is this the inn?" The words "my dear," which were spoken with homey emphasis, rasped in the father's ear, but he made no comment.

"Here, here," the driver said, indicating with his hand. His tone of voice had something of the whinny of a horse.

"Take down the luggage," the father ordered the driver. The driver loosened the rope, but not without showing his resentment at the order. The son and the daughter stood there, bleary from the bumpy ride, the arguments, and the clear air.

"We're here," said the mother, as though there were something new in that statement. It was an overcast day, yet it was still possible to sense the great height of the tall trees, and their jarring contrast to the squat houses.

"Are there empty rooms?" The father spoke self-importantly.

"There are, thank God." The innkeeper spoke in a low voice. The father hated his face, but more than that he was annoyed by the addition of those words "thank God."

"We need three rooms," he shouted as though speaking to a deaf man.

"We have them, sir. How many are you?"

"Four."

"Two rooms will be enough for you. The rooms are big, spacious, as you shall see immediately with your own eyes."

"We need three," the father insisted, so the man would know who was making the decisions.

"As you wish," said the landlord.

The rooms were wide, with beamed ceilings. The furniture was sparse, not fancy, made of local materials: oak, reeds, and linen. Rugs lay on the floor and walls. "Where is the bathroom?" asked the father.

"The bathtub is here," said the landlord. "But the toilet is downstairs, in a sheltered place."

"What poverty." The father did not conceal his discontent.

"To my regret there is neither electricity nor running water here. We draw water from the well." The man did not sound apologetic.

"And how much is it?"

The landlord named a sum. The price was not high.

The mother's impression was different. She was pleased with the place, but because her husband was angry, she refrained from expressing her opinion. She stood by the window. The dread and oppression of recent days lessened in her. All at once the silence and smell of the water recalled the memory of other, distant times—returning home for holidays, her father's and mother's faces.

In the meantime the driver brought up the suitcases. The father paid. The embarrassment of the first moments was dispelled and the innkeeper approached the guests and announced: "The table is set." In fact he had delegated command to his wife, a woman of about forty whose face still retained some marks of beauty. She welcomed them in Yiddish.

The table was laden with good food—cheese, butter, and sour cream. Coffee in the pot. "Marvelous," said the daughter, widening her eyes, as though she were not speaking of a supper table but rather of something precious. They ate without speaking. The table was old-fashioned, round, but it seemed that the daughter was sitting at the head, perhaps because her eyes were open so wide, as though trying to soak up the entire sight. The mother was intent on pacifying her husband. The coffee did not suit him.

Felix was an orderly man. Anything illogical made him distraught. He suffered whenever something was convoluted. He knew only of directness and clarity. The meetings over which he presided never lasted longer than an hour. The people under him knew they had to get to the undisguised essence of a problem. Now this trip, the bumps and the filth. He had opposed this caprice with all his soul. For weeks Henrietta had besieged his heart. Finally, against his will, they had set out. Now he was overcome with weariness, the forgotten fury, and revulsion. He disliked the coffee. Henrietta's explanations, that chicory improved the taste, were of no avail. He insisted: the coffee was watery.

"Is something missing?" asked the innkeeper's wife.

"Everything is fine, very tasty." Henrietta spoke in the innkeeper's wife's tongue. For the first time Felix heard his wife speaking the Jews' language. He was appalled, and an involuntary smile tightened his lips.

"What are we going to do here?" the son Karl asked. He was sixteen, lanky, hairy, and entirely preoccupied with himself: his body and his clothing. He was not a good student. Without the aid of private tutors he would have been suspended from the gymnasium. He gave no thought to that shame. Soccer exhilarated him to the point of drunkenness. The mother would shield him: "He's still a boy, he'll change, it's hard for him, he has his own needs." A year earlier it had become clear: he would not finish gymnasium; he would soon have to transfer to one of those workshops called vocational schools. The disgrace was acute.

The daughter was different. From childhood she had spoken little. She sat quietly for hours. Even then her glance had an alien sharpness. When she grew older that gravity had not faded from her eyes. The teachers liked her manners and diligence. The father's pride was boundless. Soon she proved to be precise too, a lover of order, and ambitious. She would sit at the piano and practice for hours. The results were very good, not superlative. In her heart the mother was pleased: no one lives beyond his years, too much effort is bad for your health, better to play for your own enjoyment than in a concert hall. She did not dare to express those thoughts except to herself. She knew the father pinned high hopes on his daughter.

7

After finishing gymnasium some anguished lines had appeared on Helga's face. At first it seemed like a passing mood, but in time the lines proved to be etched in and permanent. For hours she would sit in an armchair without uttering a sound. Her white face lost its freshness. Like crows, doctors darkened the house. Afterward, from corridor to corridor, from office to office, there was no prominent physician at whose doors they failed to knock. They went as far away as Switzerland. Strangely, Helga never complained. She was obedient, as though she understood that this was her duty now. Her obedience was complete and frightening.

The shock was strong. Her father lost interest in his business. All his thoughts were bent on Helga's condition, and the more he thought, the more he became convinced that the doctors were witless frauds. The best of them were powerless to help. Helga sank ever deeper into herself. Sometimes it seemed like braving dark waters, and sometimes like empty passivity.

The mother quietly accepted Helga's fate, perhaps because she had grown up in a home with many children, misfortunes, and illnesses. For hours she would sit with Helga, talking to her, and on the days she refused to eat, the mother fed her with a spoon. She took care of her with simplicity, as she had when she was an infant. The father couldn't stand that. After a day of hard work he would go out to a coffeehouse like some poor soul and play chess.

Yet the business did not suffer. On the contrary, there

was some growth. The father would travel from place to place. Everyone was amazed at his distractedness, his generosity, that a man of his stature would sometimes sit in a simple tavern.

Helga's beauty did not fade in her time of disease. Though she ate too much her face wasn't marred. Sometimes her illness wasn't noticeable. She would sit straight at the table, ask serious questions, and take part in the discussion.

"What's the matter with you, Helga?"

"I don't know. Why do you ask?"

"We want to help you."

"You don't have to. I feel fine."

That answer frightened him more than anything. He was used to thinking in clear terms, and not only about money matters. Now it was as though his hands were shackled.

While sorrow still gnawed at them, the mother heard a rumor that far away, in the Carpathians, there was a miracle-working healer. That rumor evoked a powerful echo in her soul. Since her childhood she had been drawn to the Carpathians. Her ancestors had come from there, and in her old age her mother had spoken of her birthplace with great yearning.

Felix rejected the proposal angrily. He would no longer chase moonbeams. The local pagan doctors were more than enough. "We won't go to the old sorcerers." The matter was brought up several times. The father did not, for some reason, use the term "superstition," which he frequently did, but rather "savage belief." One evening the mother said, "Nevertheless, I would like to try the healer."

"If you wish, let's go."

"My heart tells me that the healer won't fail us."

"If those are your feelings, let's go."

"And what do you think?"

"I don't like the idea."

"In that case, I won't impose my will."

Weeks passed. The clouds departed from above the city and the whole sky was bared in its blue splendor. The tardy summer finally arrived. It broke out on every tree, and thousands of leaves suddenly covered the naked branches. The light celebrated everything.

Helga felt better. Laughter even returned and blossomed on her lips. In the afternoons she would sit at the piano and play. Sounds came back and filled the rooms with hope. The father's joy was boundless. For a month the joy continued, as long as the bright days. Then, for no apparent reason, she closed the windows, wrapped herself in a blanket, and declared: "I'm cold." The sparkle in her eyes dimmed. The old doctor who came to see her said, "It's come again." He spoke to himself, in great despair. The father, who had intended to raise a fuss, said nothing. That very night he announced surprisingly, "I give up."

"What?" said the mother. She knew that it was no easy thing for him. Tears streamed down her cheeks.

"Don't cry." His old voice came back to him.

Strangely, now that he had agreed, she was in no rush to pack. Fear gripped her too. The Carpathians seemed far away to her, wind-scoured and wild. The father's silent agreement only made that vision more powerful to her. She put off the departure from day to day.

Finally Helga herself made the decision. "Why aren't we going to the Carpathians?" she asked.

"If you wish, we'll go," said the mother. She was glad the request had come from her daughter.

They left in early autumn. As soon as they left, Felix wrapped himself in his overcoat and refused to speak. In vain Henrietta tried to make him say something. "If it's against your will, let's go back. We can go back. We haven't gone far."

Felix did not answer. He withdrew imperceptibly into slumber. For hours he slept, his mouth tight, his arms crossed on his chest. Every button of his coat was closed. When he awoke the train had already sped to the last stop. High mountains surrounded the cars. Trees in every shade of green darkened the windows.

"Where are we?" he asked.

"Not far."

"How do you know?"

"I heard. The conductor went by an hour ago."

"And you believe him," he said and shut his eyes again.

"Father is very tired, isn't he?" She spoke to her sick daughter for some reason.

"Father needs absolute repose," answered Helga.

Henrietta was frightened by her use of the word "absolute," which sounded like the decree of fate to her.

That evening the train stopped. They stood in the cold station, exposed to the wind, the yard teeming with peasants. Felix lost his practicality in that hubbub. "Where are we? Where are we?" he fumbled as though in a nightmare. Henrietta went from one person to another, asking. Finally she stood on the cold platform and bargained with the drivers, who claimed the destination was far off, the way dangerous, and now, in this season, the wheels were liable to be stuck in the mud.

Felix did not intervene in the bargaining, but he noticed: the wildness of the place did not frighten Henrietta. She spoke simply to the husky drivers. The few words of Ruthenian she had learned at home served her well.

The journey to the mountain took three days. They crossed forests, narrow bridges, and deserted mountain peaks. It was like a bad dream, with all the colors of a bad dream. Helga vomited and Karl complained of headaches. Felix sat in the corner and never ceased blaming himself. If a man leaves his home and journeys into the desert, he is guilty. Only the guilty run away. What are we seeking here? Whom are we looking for here?

Several times the driver stopped the coach and announced: "I'm not going farther unless you pay me a bonus." Henrietta was not fazed. She would bargain with him, offering a certain sum. Finally he would agree and start again. Thus, the carriage worked its way upward, climbing from peak to peak.

Strangely, Felix was not pleased with her resourcefulness. It seemed to him his wife was deceiving him. That unclean feeling made him forget the travails of the journey, and Helga. His selfishness and fears flooded him once again.

II

ON THE NEXT DAY the sky cleared and they stood before the inn, near two tall oaks rising broadly above them. The pungent smell of water filled the air. The settlement consisted of a single street, not a long one. At the end of it, the forests, the rush of water, and the lowing of cattle. Not far off, in a clearing, stood the shaded dairy. It turned out that they even sold homemade ice cream from a counter. Helga's face glowed. She savored the delicacy, and when she finished she asked for more.

The mother was glad. The father never took his eyes off his daughter. He had spent long hours with her, sometimes in conversation, sometimes in silence. She was no longer herself. Even when she left her prison for a moment, it was no longer the same Helga. Her laughter, like her gloom, frightened him.

"What do we do now?"

"I suggest we look at the forest," said Henrietta in a domestic tone. She said it simply as she used to speak when they arrived at their vacation house.

For a moment that tone of hers made Felix forget their reason for coming here. The whole thing seemed to him like an error that would soon clear up on its own. "Don't worry," he wanted to say, but he immediately remembered that the autumn was at its height, the roads were in bad repair, and it was doubtful whether any carter would agree to bring them back to the railroad; meanwhile at home, the business was vulnerable with no one keeping an eye on it.

Henrietta followed his thoughts tensely, finally saying, "Come on, children, forward." She meant to exorcise the shades haunting her husband.

Afterward they parted ways. The father took the main branch with Karl, while the mother and Helga returned to the inn. For a long time the father walked without saying anything. His son, who had grown very tall in the past year, made him feel awkward with his bulk. Secretly he sought to avoid being with him.

"Do you like this place?" he finally asked.

"No," came the short answer. He apparently sensed the impersonality of his father's question.

"Why not?"

"The greenery desolates me." Strangely the word "greenery," which was only meant to indicate that silent vastness, surprised the father. He didn't believe his son was capable of saying anything except in the most ordinary way.

"Doesn't the greenery delight the eye?"

"Delight the eye." Karl repeated his words. Felix imagined he heard slight mockery of that rhetorical figure in his son's voice.

"Nothing satisfies you."

"I'm not satisfied with doing nothing."

For a moment the father looked at his son, a head taller than himself, as though he wished to appease him. "We're waiting here. True, it isn't an easy wait. It will soon be over."

"Always somebody or something, but no one thinks of me."

"What do you lack?"

"Doing what I want."

"What do you want?"

"Not to be here."

The last words, spoken in a kind of blunt directness, left no further doubt in the father's mind that the boy had suffered for years, and now it was only right to placate him. With what? He did not know. "If that's your desire, we shall do as you wish. You know we didn't come here for pleasure."

"The burden falls on me. I always suffer."

"From what? From what?" The father drew nearer to him. He had not thought this wild weed had words of its own.

"I suffer from everything: at school, at home, during vacations in pensions, from all this idleness that ends in long conversations."

"But your sister is sick, isn't she?"

16

"Ever since I remember in the house: 'Don't make any noise, Helga is doing homework.' 'Helga is playing piano.' 'Helga is studying for a test.' You drove her crazy."

"We?" the father fixed him with a defensive look in his eyes.

"You turned her into a Jewish weakling."

"Why?" The son's brevity infected the father somewhat.

"You drove her crazy."

"Jewish weakling"—he had probably picked that up at school. He certainly did not understand the meaning of the words.

"I hate those Jewish weaklings," the son grumbled.

"What harm did they do you?"

"I don't know."

"You're Jewish yourself." The father tried to show him his error.

Evening gradually fell. The last sunlight clung to the treetops. The rush of the water in the brooks grew louder. "On the other side of the mountain it's raining hard," the thought passed through the father's mind. Three years ago, he recalled, Karl had asked to be registered at the military academy, but for some reason the father had decreed that it was not to be. The mother, to her credit, had not rejected her son's desire, but since the father was angry, she refrained from intervening. The matter was set aside and forgotten. Karl was registered in a gymnasium.

At first it seemed he was keeping up. Soon it was

clear he was not only having trouble with algebra and Latin, but grammar too was not one of his strong points. On the playing fields it was a different story: there his legs moved swiftly. He was the star forward of the soccer team. That glory did not shield him from expulsion.

They walked along the dirt road without exchanging a word. Momentarily Felix forgot the trials of the journey and Helga's illness. He was pained by the words his son had hurled at him. Since the boy had been small, Felix had to admit, he had not been fond of him, he had not wanted to be close to him; he had seen him as a kind of creature belonging entirely to his wife, to the healthy, practical people who don't get overexcited, who think in simple terms, digging into life and enjoying whatever comes to hand. Now Karl came and slapped him in the face—"I'm your son. Healthy people also have a right to live. True, health isn't excessive sensitivity, but neither is it dark crudeness." Thoughts streamed through his mind, and he was put off by them. Karl, athletically striding at his side, only heightened his fear.

When they drew near the inn, the night was already full. The street was broad and empty. A saddled horse stood at the door. No one was there, only silence spreading out, thick and dark. Helga met them at the door and said, "Where were you?"

"We took a walk; it was very pleasant." As he said it, the melody of past days returned to him, when Helga had been healthy and vacations had been taken in orderly fashion. Who would have guessed that a hidden enemy was secretly undermining them.

"Helga—" He tried to break through the thick barrier.

"Father." She stretched out her hands.

Later a dairy meal was served. They were all hungry and ate the plentiful food served by the innkeeper's wife. They sat over dinner till it grew quite late.

"We should have come here long ago," said the mother.

"Why?" The father was puzzled.

"The vegetables. I can taste their curative powers." There was sadness in her voice, as though she were not speaking of some trivial desire but rather of an error which could never be remedied. The darkness spread until one could feel its grains. Fatigue enveloped them like an old shepherd's cloak.

"I had a long conversation with Karl," said Felix.

"I'm glad," Henrietta said.

For a moment he wanted to approach his wife. In the past months they had hardly spoken, only practical words, and few of those. Estrangement stood between them. Even Helga's illness failed to bring them together. On the contrary, old sores that had closed long ago now opened again. He tried to open his heart slightly, but she only recoiled and said, "Good night."

III

THE NEXT DAY they rose early and went to the healer. Karl stayed back at the inn. It was about eight o'clock, and wisps of fog hovered over the somnolent heights. The light was scant and dim. Felix, for some reason, spoke at length about his military service in an isolated camp in Moravia. Helga was lively and asked for details. Henrietta was surprised to find her husband so talkative. Ever since she had known him he had been miserly with words.

They advanced slowly alongside orchards. The autumn had stripped the trees of their foliage. They stood low and gloomy; the fallen leaves lay at their feet ingloriously, weightless piles of rust stirred by every breeze.

Only now did Felix notice that Henrietta was wearing a kerchief on her head. She took broad strides, as though she were familiar with the place. Helga held her arm and stepped forward with her.

"Haven't we lost the way?" Felix asked.

"No," said Henrietta without turning around. "This is a well-trodden path." That expression, spoken out loud, grated in his ear, but he made no comment. The path was dry. Not much rain had fallen that night, and the earth had soaked it up.

When they reached the healer's dwelling, women, old men, and children were already gathered around the gate. They were sitting at some distance from it, resting on their bundles. Evidently they had arrived very early. Henrietta turned to one of the women. "Is this the healer's dwelling?"

"The holy man," the woman corrected her, and her bitter face grew more bitter.

The courtyard extended to the edge of the forest, but the people sat withdrawn, each in his own corner, near the gate. The children whimpered; every once in a while they would be punished with a slap or a spank, and they would grow quiet. Felix did not understand the woman's answer, but her look told him it was an angry and haughty reply. Henrietta recoiled but was undaunted. Her face grew more resolute.

"Is this the healer's residence?" asked Helga.

"Apparently," said Felix.

"Strange."

"What's strange?"

"It looks like the court of the Catholic hospital."

There too poor sick people had crowded together, mostly lepers whom the municipal hospitals refused to accommodate. The old nuns used to treat them harshly.

"It's different, completely different," said Felix without looking at her face.

"Where do we register?" Henrietta dared to ask a young woman who was hugging a baby.

"No need." Her face shone.

"Can one speak with him?"

"Certainly. As much as you wish. Why don't you sit down?" The woman spoke softly as though she were not talking of misery but rather a passing distress that time would cure. The oaks cast heavy shadows on the courtyard, but it was not dark, perhaps because the front of the house had been whitewashed recently. The smell of whitewash filled the air.

"I'm not from here." Henrietta spoke to her in Yiddish as one speaks to a friend.

"Where are you from?" The woman was surprised.

"From Vienna."

"Good Lord, you're from Vienna!" A kind of astonishment filled the young woman's eyes. "And you came to see our holy man."

"We heard a lot about him."

"It's good you came. I'm already like family here. My husband died a year ago and since then I've had nothing but woe," she said and immediately, without formality, she offered them a cornmeal cake filled with plums. The pastry still smelled warm from the oven.

"Excellent," said Henrietta. Helga knelt to express her mute gratitude. Felix noticed: deep lines crossed the young woman's face.

From this angle the sight was far from splendid. A few old men wrapped in tattered coats lay on the ground and muttered in broken voices. Sometimes it sounded like prayer.

"What are they doing? Are they praying?" Felix asked.

"I don't know, believe me," Henrietta said very emotionally, for some reason.

Helga stood quietly. Her face was covered by the broad collar of her coat. Unlike her brother she was shorter than her father and mother, also thinner, and now, standing between them, she seemed extremely perplexed.

Felix lit a cigarette. His thin contempt, familiar to Henrietta, had changed. Lines of hidden sadness wove themselves over his face. Occasionally a man would get up and go to the gate, standing next to it as though expecting it to open. The man's obstinate stance only confirmed that the gate was truly locked.

"Won't you have a cup of milk?" the young woman asked.

"No thank you," said Henrietta. "We had something to drink before we came here."

"Too bad," said the woman. The baby began to wail, and she hugged it and hid it in her broad bosom. Henrietta was astounded by the way she held the baby, as though she wished to shield it not only with her body

23

but with her whole being. "That is not how children are raised in Vienna. That is not how I raised my children." The thought pierced her mind.

The baby calmed down and the woman went back to her place. She poured herself a cup of milk and broke off a piece of bread, sitting down with her legs crossed. The strong lines on her face softened a little, and she was alone with herself. Helga's eyes never left her.

After about an hour the sun cut through the thicket of trees and filled the clearing with light. One of the old men got to his feet, approached the gate, and knocked on it. As there was no answer he pounded on the boards with his two bony fists. For a while he stood and pounded. No one said anything, perhaps because he stood erect and resolute. Women spread cloths out on the ground and prepared meals. The starched, white cloths brought out their faces in relief as they ate: long faces with a kind of sadness crusted over their eyes. Helga smiled, as though she recognized sisters in suffering.

In one corner three men stood apart. They spoke loudly, with many hand motions. They were talking about a horse for sale, which was tied to a tree trunk. The beast stood wearily and without expression. After bargaining, a short, older man bought it. He was pleased with his purchase but took care not to show it. The sellers were also pleased. They counted the money and divided it evenly.

Felix stood and observed them with a long look, following their rapidly shifting motions. The sight amused him. For a moment he exchanged his ironic expression for soft laughter. The men were so involved in their business they did not perceive his stare.

The buyer untied the horse and said, "I'm going," as though to see whether they regretted the bargain.

"Go in peace," said the sellers as one man.

In the afternoon a cloud descended on the clearing. The people's faces filled with weariness and the words they exchanged grew ever fewer. Now it seemed as though slumber were about to envelop them all together. Henrietta, for some reason, expected the woman to ask her why they had come. The woman did not ask. She handed her two pears and said, "Have some."

"Thank you," said Henrietta, taking the fruit from her hands. "When shall we be fortunate enough to see the healer?"

"I don't know. The gate isn't opened every day."

"Why?" asked Henrietta.

"That's the way it is." The cloud still darkened the yard, while an old man rose to his feet. First it seemed as though he wished to approach the gate, but he did not do so. He stood in one place and closed his eyes. The noise suddenly abated and silence fell on the place.

"Whence comest thou?" the man began without ceremony, with the sound of a prayer.

"From a stinking droplet," the other old men answered loudly.

"Whither goest thou?" he continued.

"To a place of dust, rot, and worms," they answered thunderously.

"Before whom wilt thou render an accounting?"

"Before the King of Kings, the Holy One blessed be He."

For a moment the voices died down, and directly they began chanting: "Keep three things in view and thou shalt not fall into sin." Power was in the old men's voices. The gloomy clearing suddenly filled with warmth and closeness. The chant rose again and soared in many tones. The children's crying no longer disturbed anyone. Boisterously they rolled in the dust as though in their own yards.

For two full hours the song continued and the words were filled with a new essence. At last the melody sank down, retracted, grew round, became a silence. For some reason that mighty song inspired a thirst in the people. They raised glases and nibbled brown cakes, calling to each other, "Lechayim, lechayim."

While the free drinking continued, the gate opened and a man of average height stood in it, his rumpled look showing total absentmindedness. He immediately called out, without apologies or formalities, "Go home. The holy man did not leave his room. He is ill." A great uproar ensued; the people grumbled, but no one raised his hand. But pride overcame the bitter woman, and she shouted, outraged, "Now you tell us?"

"What can I do?" said the attendant with a helpless gesture.

"Shame!" she flashed.

"I'm only the attendant." He shrugged his shoulders as though used to humiliation.

"A human life's not worth a farthing to you." She picked up her bundle, and with a movement conveying great contempt, she hurried away. Others, in contrast, approached the attendant and asked for details. He scattered the barrage of their words in every direction.

A tall, thin man, brought out of his corner by the sudden announcement, went straight up to the attendant. " 'Truth shall grow from the earth,' isn't that what we say?" He spoke softly.

"Correct," answered the attendant absentmindedly. "What's the connection?"

"All the more, what does that mean? What does that mean?"

"Ask the holy man, don't ask me."

"It isn't self-evident. It's a difficult verse, isn't it."

"There are more than enough difficulties." The attendant dismissed him with a frightfully matter-of-fact tone.

The man's face burned with shame, and he froze in his place. For a moment he looked about him with a trembling glance, as though he were among alien and hostile people. His tall stature shrank, and he withdrew into his shadowy corner, which now lay in darkness.

The day ended and thin evening lights filtered through the thick foliage. The smell of water and hyssop filled the air.

For a moment Felix forgot the ignominy of his coming there. His eyes were gripped by the people as they gradually dispersed. He forgot himself. Henrietta, constantly seeking to console her daughter, said out loud, "No matter. We'll come tomorrow. There's no hurry."

Helga's face withdrew further into her broad collar. "We're going back to the inn, right?" she asked.

Felix hurried out of the clearing. The nighttime lights sparkled in the darkness, red and cold. No wind blew. All the sights of the courtyard stood before his eyes as though they had congealed. The young woman hugging the infant at her breast, the tall, thin man who had sought the meaning of an obscure verse. The attendant thronged by many people, poor and miserable, who had reviled him shamelessly. Strange, no one had defended him, as though he were fair game. For some reason Felix felt sorry for that stranger. In point of fact he felt sorry for himself, for at such an untimely moment, in such obscure circumstances, he had left his house and set out for this exposed, alien land. It was not solely Henrietta's fault. He himself had promoted this illusion. As in a nightmare he knew his guilt, he knew the defenses, but his mouth was blocked. Again, as though in a dream, with utter clarity, he saw the two days which had passed on that isolated height. He saw the inn, the road, and the way to the healer's dwelling. He continued, and the sights were divested of their earthly light, and another, pure light illumined the faces of the people waiting in that courtyard clearing. He had to admit to a powerful feeling of submissiveness. Felix knew that people don't change, the body is firm and demands its due, fears are many, the desire to be good is no pure desire; nevertheless he felt that he had been overtaken by a new darkness.

"Felix, we must turn to the right."

He heard Henrietta's voice and snapped awake. They were standing at the doorway of the inn. In the hall kerosene lamps diffused an old, forgotten warmth. The innkeeper's wife greeted them pleasantly but without unnecessary posturing. Henrietta sat by her side and told her they had waited for hours until finally they were told that the healer himself was ill and had not left his room. The innkeeper's wife listened to every word that left Henrietta's lips and immediately went to the kitchen to prepare supper.

Karl, it appeared, had spent the time pleasantly. He had bowled in the tavern. His face was red and his shirt spotted with sweat. His entire presence at the table expressed appetite and hunger. The black bread broke easily in his hands. He dipped the pieces in a plate of sour cream. Felix looked at him very closely, and as he looked, he saw the sequence of events that had taken place during the past year with cold clarity.

Henrietta sat very close to Helga and spoke to her softly. Helga was pleased with her mother's closeness. She told her at uncustomary length about her last matriculation examination in mathematics, how she had managed to remember the correct formula, but one error, a fatal one, had spoiled everything. Clearly, even though the examination had taken place three years ago, that mistake still rankled. Henrietta said, "You were always good in mathematics. No one can take that talent away from you." In that way she won her over immediately. Helga laughed. Felix, listening to the conversation, was envious that Helga was speaking to Henrietta with entire trust. "She has stopped speaking to me." The thought grated in his mind.

In the meantime Karl lapped up everything within reach, sour cream, cheese, and eggs, as though his appetite knew no bounds. It was hard for Felix to bear that clumsy face, but still he wished to say, "Pardon me, son, pardon me, for the bad feeling seething inside me. You are good. You are simple. The way people ought to be. I'm the one who should be beaten."

IV

THE NEXT MORNING they rose early and found, to their surprise, that no one was in the healer's courtyard. It was quiet, and the gate was open. Bread crumbs left for the birds remained on the tree stumps. Aside from that, no sign. The morning light was faint but not dark. The smell of moist decay was in the air. Felix went up and knocked at the open gate.

"Come in," a voice was heard from within. It was the attendant. He stood near a beam, bent over, perusing a newspaper. A thin wrinkle of irony clung to his absent-minded face, the look that anyone acquires after years of standing at a gate, accepting and rejecting.

"No one is here today." For some reason Henrietta expressed her surprise out loud.

"Have no fear," said the attendant in an old-fashioned way, like a merchant. "They'll come yet."

"We were here yesterday, and we're trying our luck again. Is the holy man feeling better?"

"Much better, thank God. Where are you from?"

"Vienna."

Hearing that word, the attendant smiled as though savoring a special taste. "How can I assist you?"

"We have come to see the holy man." Henrietta spoke in a low voice.

"No problem." The man spoke in dialect. "Be seated."

"Must we register? Excuse me. We don't know how things are done."

"No need for anything." He smiled again. His smile immediately laid bare the thin line between matter and spirit. The corridor was illuminated by two narrow windows, and the smell of mildew stood in the air. The walls were undecorated. Two benches lay along their length, and a rustic sideboard.

"Why won't you sit down?" said the attendant. "I cannot serve you anything, the driver didn't bring any wood, and the oven is cold. If you aren't tough, people have no mercy on you. The drivers can't be trusted, they don't keep their word. In the meantime the house has gotten cold."

"No need. We aren't thirsty." Henrietta sought to appease him.

"The drivers don't keep their word, that's their nature, even with regular customers. We are regular customers of theirs, once a week, like clockwork, a medium-sized wagon full of logs." He went to the sideboard and opened the middle drawer, as though to remove something from it. The drawer came out easily and revealed its contents: a supply of used books. But that wasn't what he was looking for. He pushed the drawer back in with both hands, using his right shoulder too.

"Two years ago a couple came here from abroad, nice people." The attendant tried to fit his tongue to German pronunciation. "How much does the trip from Vienna cost?"

Henrietta named an amount.

"A pretty penny. By the way, who told you about the holy man?"

"We heard a lot about him, from many people."

"I understand." Over the years a few Jews had found their way there from the faraway cities. They were always well dressed, erect, and proud. The attendant, like any poor man, burdened with many children, behaved deferentially before an erect posture and fine clothing. But he never put out his hand to ask for charity. At one time he had been secretly contemptuous of their alien appearance. In recent years his own faith had not been exalted. Fear of being needy had made him into an affable man.

Henrietta wanted to ask for more details, but in her embarrassment, perhaps because of the man's practical appearance, her questions deserted her. Felix stood at a distance from them, listening. Anger seethed within him. Mainly to contradict his wife's words, he wanted to get up and shout: "We don't believe, and we are not the children of believers." If it weren't for the man's miserable appearance, his clothes and short stature, he would have stood up and pushed him into the corridor, saying to him what he had heard in his childhood more than once: "Filthy Jew." The man looked so thin and woebegone that the thought of even brushing against him revolted Felix. He wanted just one thing, to get out of there as fast as possible.

"I shall see if the holy man is free," the attendant whispered, almost mischievously.

Helga removed her head from the broad collar. Her pale face was somewhat calmer. Once again it expressed some wonderment: "When will we see the doctor?"

"He isn't a doctor, daughter, but a healer."

Hearing that word, Helga opened her eyes even wider.

Felix's gaze no longer left Helga's face. The sorrow he had hidden within himself for two full years had penetrated to his bones. He felt tension in his leg muscles and cold in his arms. "Why are we dragging the girl from place to place?" he thought. "Now this strangeness, this dampness." Without knowing what he was doing he got up and shook his legs. Henrietta, whose eyes had been cast down all that time, raised them as though to silence the noise, but Felix preempted her and fixed her with an angry stare.

From the nearby rooms silence flowed, as though

they were as empty of household goods as the corridor. A few flies bumped between the double windows and buzzed restlessly.

"He's different. He's a healer." For some reason Henrietta made an effort to explain to her daughter again.

"He's religious, isn't he."

"Yes, you're right." She spoke to her as one speaks to a little girl.

Felix looked at his watch. The cigarette between his fingers trembled. Henrietta wanted to say, "Soon," but she restrained herself. For months she had spoken to her husband only about practical things, and even then in brief. True, Helga's illness had dispelled some of the estrangement, as though they realized that the dearest thing of all lay beyond the confines of their distance from each other. Caution in choice of words remained as before. Not to get too close, to gain the children's grace.

"It's cold, isn't it?" Helga said.

"Not much longer," the mother said with false assurance.

Once Helga's vocabulary had been full and rich, but since her illness it had shrunk. She used words of one or two syllables, as though the long words had been lost to her. "It's cold, isn't it?" she repeated.

Felix's patience was wearing thin. He now paced back and forth along the corridor. The wooden floor bent with each of his strides. Henrietta sat without moving, as if she wished to soak up the noise of his irritable pacing.

"Enter," a voice was finally heard.

They rose as one. Henrietta took the lead, Helga after her, and Felix at some distance. It was a short corridor with two lighted openings at the end. "Where do we enter?" Henrietta asked in a whisper. "Here," a soft voice answered.

The sight revealed to their eyes was astonishing in its simplicity and nakedness. A smallish room, lit by two narrow windows. A few shelves with books and a low bed. At the table sat an old man leaning over a book. "Come in." The white-haired man raised his head. "Sit down, children, sit down." He spoke softly, as though to relatives.

"Where are you Jews from?"

"From Vienna," Henrietta hurriedly replied.

"A large city for the Lord," the old man said, and a sparkle flashed through his blue eyes. "Welcome."

"We came to seek a cure." Henrietta went right to the point.

"You came to seek a cure from flesh and blood?"

Henrietta lowered her eyes. She had rehearsed that sentence to herself all along the way and had not imagined it would be found wanting.

"Flesh and blood are merely flesh and blood." The old man spoke in a singsong, and as though to illustrate, he put down his hand, thin and white. The bones showed through the wrapping of transparent skin. "The Creator of the world is great, and He will bring a cure to the sick among His people."

Felix gazed at the old man with a narrow, skeptical

36

stare. He had not understood the phrase "flesh and blood," and anyway the whole conversation sounded utterly fallacious to him. The old man apparently felt Felix's skeptical stare, but he ignored it. He knew those city folk well. More than once they had dragged him into arguments, pointless arguments about individual providence, priority and posteriority, and similar issues redolent of complaint and arrogance. The old man knew: many were stricken in the big city, and they lacked innocence. Nevertheless he locked his door to no one. On the contrary, he felt a kind of hidden attraction for those souls.

"What is the girl's name?" he asked Henrietta.

"Helga," Henrietta whispered.

"Hasn't she a Jewish name?"

"I am grieved to say no." Henrietta lowered her head.

"What's the matter with that name?" Felix leaped up.

The old man did not respond. Henrietta hurriedly explained: "My late mother was named Tsirl. She was born in this region, and she moved to Vienna when she was young. My mother suffered greatly in the big city and all those years she longed to return to the land of her childhood. She died many years ago. I couldn't give my daughter her name. That name is uncommon in Vienna. I was afraid people would laugh at her. Was I wrong?"

Now it seemed that Felix was about to get up and make a statement, but he did not. He straightened his upper body like someone restraining himself from responding to an injustice.

The old man closed his eyes. Not many people came to him from the capital, and the few who did were desperate and came unwillingly. The winds of despair bore them to him. When he was young contention had renewed his zeal, but in recent years the struggle had become hard for him. He hadn't the strength to sail out of his body and cleave to people's despair. His ulcer too, in the last months, had tortured him without letup, and in the cold season the pains became sharper. They no longer let him take leave of himself. They locked him into his sickly body.

If only he could shut himself off, cling to his books, no longer see anyone, return his soul to the Creator in serenity, without rushing. Haste was unseemly. But what could he do? The world knew no mercy: give us advice, give us a cure, give us a blessing. And those attendants, flushed with greed. If he could, he would send them all away from him. He shook himself free of his thoughts, angry that he had let them take control, and turned to those sitting before him.

"My mother, may she rest in peace, was named Tsirl. My daughter was born two years after her death. That name isn't acceptable in Vienna. Everybody would have laughed at her. Very Jewish. Very conspicuous. Everyone would have tormented her." As she said it she felt the old sin, which she had hidden away in her soul, rising up and emerging. If Helga had been called Tsirl, Henrietta's mother would certainly have protected her.

The old man did not respond to that argument.

Felix's gnawing eyes disturbed him. He felt that the man was standing above him like a prosecutor. "And where do you live?" The old man forgot he had already asked.

"In Vienna, sir," Henrietta said, immediately regretting she had said "sir."

"It is difficult for people to live in large cities. Is it not true that trees are the most faithful of friends?"

Felix smiled to himself. He had not expected to hear such a saying from the old man.

Meanwhile the attendant entered the room. In that space he seemed even shorter. He walked about as in a poor dwelling where no one notes who comes and goes. "I don't know where I left the prayerbooks," he muttered.

Henrietta was afraid that the matter for which she had come would slip out of sight, so she spoke directly and out loud. "Our daughter needs a complete cure."

"Together with all the sick Jews," the old man added.

Henrietta did not understand the meaning of that correction, and she said, "What shall we do? What shall we do?"

"Let us pray, is it so hard to pray? Let us draw close to the holy letters and look at them."

"I have forgotten," she said, baring yet another shame. In her childhood her mother had taught her the Hebrew letters, and on holidays she used to take her to the synagogue. It was a poor synagogue without splendor. The women spoke aloud in Yiddish.

But the place had seemed like an enchanted island to her, perhaps because she did not understand a word. A light imbued those few hours beside her mother.

Her mother had died when she was young, and she stopped going to synagogue. The letters were gradually erased from her memory, but not entirely. On memorial days she would look at the prayerbook, inherited from her mother, and recite "Hear, O Israel" out loud. That hasty review and reading out loud used to conjure up her mother's face as though by magic, and the feeling that the separation would not last forever.

"I forgot." She roused from her thoughts. "Through my own fault. I ought to have prayed."

"No matter. You can learn. It's never too late."

"Who will teach us?" she said, and a kind of involuntary smile spread out on her lips.

"Nothing is easier," said the old man. "The soul is hungry for the letters."

"Why isn't he talking about Helga's sickness?" The thought passed through Felix's mind, but before he could answer he rose to his feet and said, "The matter must be clear, we are Jews but not believers, if one might put it that way."

At those words a thin, ironic smile spread across the old man's face, trembling on his lips as though to say, "Why, then, if that is so, did you come to bother an old man?" But he knew better than to ensnare a person in his own sorrow, and he lowered his head, not forgetting his self-worth, and he said, as the Jews do, "What's the connection?"

"What does he want?" Felix asked Henrietta's assistance.

Henrietta's eyes were cast down, and she did not catch Felix's cry.

"We want medical advice. If he has none, let him not delude us."

The old man's blue eyes opened slightly, and a thin, ironic smile once again flickered on his lips. "We are but flesh and blood. One cannot demand the impossible from flesh and blood." He sought to mollify Felix.

"I didn't ask for that." Felix retreated slightly. "We want clear answers. If there are none, let us be told, and we will respect your candor."

Hearing those words, the old man shut his eyes and murmured, "What can we say? It is written: not with haste, let us wait with forbearance. Forbearance." The old man emphasized his words.

But precisely those words, which were meant only to calm him down, exasperated Felix, and he called out: "We have no time. We left a house behind, business, the children need to go to school. We've lost enough."

Henrietta's face grew paler. Every word her husband uttered embarrassed and mortified her. It seemed to her that not words but vulgarities were coming from his mouth. "Be quiet," she wanted to shout, but as always she swallowed her words and said nothing. An unpleasant silence took over the room. It was evi-

41

dent to her that the old man had been insulted by Felix's words, and now he no longer wished to see anyone. She rose to her feet, and with strength not her own she called out, "We're Jews, Jews in our hearts and souls. We have forgotten our prayers, but not our faith." Many words had sought to burst from within her. Now they choked inside her throat, and tears flooded her eyes.

"Henrietta," Felix called to quiet her. Henrietta did not heed his voice. "We're lost," she wailed softly. "No one knows how to help us. You are our last hope. Don't abandon us." Hearing those words, Felix's face contracted.

The old man closed his eyes for a moment, and it seemed as if slumber had fallen upon him, but in a short time he opened his eyes. He addressed Henrietta: "We have a great Lord in the heavens, and He shall have mercy upon His people Israel and their sick. There is nothing to fear. We are in trustworthy, devoted hands. We shall have faith from now to all eternity." The words were simple, and Felix understood them, but that understanding did not increase his confidence in the old man. On the contrary, the place felt more constricted and stifling to him.

"Bring me a prayerbook," called out the old man, putting his two pale and emaciated hands on the table. His hands shook. When the attendant failed to come, he called out again, "Did you hear what I said to you?"

"I heard," came a voice from the next room. "I'm

coming," replied the voice of an attendant who no longer hastened to do his master's bidding.

A short time passed, and the attendant placed an old prayerbook on the table. The old man did not thank him. He raised the prayerbook slightly and opened it to the second page. "These are the holy letters," he said, and as he spoke his eyes seemed to glow. "The girl must be taught these bright, holy letters. Three times a day, morning, noon, and evening." The old man closed his eyes.

Henrietta wanted to speak another word, but seeing the old man's closed eyes, she rose and turned to the door. The last, practical words and the prayerbook in her hand strengthened her all at once. For some reason Felix made a strange little bow and moved aside for Henrietta.

"May the Lord send you complete recovery," called the attendant. That blessing was obviously habitual in his mouth. Henrietta opened her purse and placed five bills on the cupboard. The attendant, seeing the substantial sum, blushed and made a bow. "May the Lord send you a full benediction," he blessed them again, this time softly. Henrietta took Helga's arm and turned toward the front door with a proud bearing.

In the meantime women had gathered in the clearing. They sat in the green corners. Seeing Henrietta and Helga, splendid in their winter garments, they whispered, "From Vienna." For some reason Henrietta turned to them and called out familiarly, "Good day." The unexpected greeting surprised the women, but they immediately recovered themselves and answered, "May the Lord on high send you good health."

The light now spread on the clearing. In the nearby glade the darkness was scattered. Moist shadows crawled on the earth and crouched near the thick tree trunks.

Felix lagged behind them saying nothing. The sights still filled him. He noted one thing: a strong line had appeared on Henrietta's neck, a kind of unwavering resolution. For a moment he withdrew and waited. But immediately fury at the attendant swelled within him. A fraud and deceiver. He very much wanted to express that opinion to Helga, but he restrained himself. He was afraid of Henrietta now; in truth he was sure she would contradict his opinion.

"Mother." Helga broke the silence.

"What, my dear?"

"The healer—" Her eyes tried to touch the secret.

"He gave us this book, it's a prayerbook." Henrietta spoke in a whisper with exaggerated emphasis. "For now he asked us to learn the Hebrew letters. You'll learn them easily."

"Is that a magic charm?" Helga wondered.

"No, my dear, I wouldn't call it a magic charm, I would say it was preparation for prayer. Prayer has its own words, and we shall learn the words of prayer."

"And what shall we ask for?"

"We shall ask for goodness."

"That's easy." Helga smiled. Evidently that painless contact was pleasant for her.

Felix walked at a distance from them. He was all tense. The words that left Henrietta's mouth pierced his ear and pained him, but seeing that Helga responded quietly, he did not intervene.

Helga's face glowed as though the sanity of old times had returned to her; her stride was straight and balanced, with measured steps, as if they were not coming from the healer's chamber but had sat in a coffeehouse for an hour, enjoying a dish of strawberries.

"Father, why are you in a hurry?" Surprisingly she addressed her father.

"I need a cup of coffee. I'm thirsty."

"If so, why don't we go to the buffet?"

"I'm cold. This coat isn't keeping me warm," Felix answered irrelevantly. All his repressed anger wanted to burst out and scream: "Frauds, they're all frauds!"

Helga's face was lit by some forgotten levity. "Father, let's go into a coffeehouse and drink coffee. Maybe we'll find good cheesecake. Afterward we'll learn to pray. There's time, isn't there?"

Those light words exasperated Felix, and he said, "We won't pray on orders, we'll pray when we feel the need. We aren't the servants of some dubious healer."

"I found the old man, how can I say it, a good-hearted person, isn't that so?"

"Perhaps. But we won't pray on orders. We have our own will. We shall not be subject to overlords." The last sentence, an absolute one, cut short Helga's speech all at once, and the few words that had been ready in her mouth were swallowed in her throat. She stood now as though rebuked.

Henrietta listened tensely. The words raked her flesh. It was hard for her to bear that vocabulary then. The estrangement that had dwelled between them for years was laid bare, utter estrangement.

V

THE NEXT DAY was cloudy, but no rain fell. Felix rose early. He shaved and washed his upper body in cold water. Without noticing it, he was drawn to take care of himself. An old feeling of pleasure increasingly gripped his body, evoking, as though by magic, his gymnasium days, the summer vacations which had extended, green, over two full months. There had been a special pleasure in the days when his parents went to a pension and left him to his own devices. For a moment he forgot he was forty-eight years old, far from his native city, from his home and business, shackled in a foreign place and a murky season. All the years vanished from his soul that morning, as though the whole thing were an illusion, a trivial caprice. Since he found it pleasant in the bathroom, he returned and perfumed

47

his face with cologne. The scent restored an old and forgotten feeling of power.

Later too, when he sat alone in the dining room, the black bread, the fresh cream, the coffee in the brown mug—that pleasant feeling did not abandon him. And when the meal was finished he retired to the well-lit foyer. The old optimism enveloped him for a moment like a warm cloak, and he wrapped himself in it. For a long time he sat by himself, with a growing feeling that the nightmare would soon be over.

Before an hour passed, Henrietta appeared in the dining room. She stood at the door, and her figure, which he knew in all its details, was entirely different, no longer that Henrietta in a soft robe, but now a woman whose intention was firm, and even when she sat at the table, spreading the bread, pouring the coffee, her firmness of will was visible. She asked the innkeeper's wife several practical questions, and it seemed to Felix, who did not understand some of the words, that the innkeeper's wife was communicating certain articles of faith to her. "In a short while I won't be here," he said to himself. Then and there he decided he would go and inquire about the train schedule and the arrangements necessary for a rapid descent from the mountain.

Still seated, he heard steps approaching him, graceful ones, Karl's. He appeared in the dining room with the lightness of an athlete, immediately taking his place at the table.

"Did you sleep well?" asked Henrietta.

"Yes." He spoke with masculine curtness.

Contact between him and his mother was easy even now. She knew he would not be drawn to faith. He was too earthly and instinctive. Prohibitions and prayers were alien to him. She used a special language to address him, simple words, the language she was accustomed to using in the grocery store, the seamstress's, or with a housemaid.

Karl ate everything that was put on his plate, and when he had finished he went out to the foyer, where he immediately discovered his father. Felix rose to his feet and said, "Will you come out with me?"

"I'm ready when you are." He spoke to his father as though to a coconspirator.

"Let's go out the back door." Not wishing to meet Henrietta, he slipped out into the woods with Karl. For a moment they looked at each other like two friends who had managed to climb over a fence and slip back with pockets full of apples. Petty theft with a smidgen of mischief.

"How was it yesterday?" asked the father.

"Fun." Karl sought to be brief.

"You won, I gather."

"That's right." A roguish spark lit Karl's eyes.

A suppressed pride, which he had never released before, flooded his heart. All those years it had been hard for him to bear the thought that his son was falling behind in his studies. He viewed that as disgraceful obstinacy, a mysterious flaw. He did not wish to hear of any advantage to that flaw, if one might call it that. Like

49

all Viennese Jews, he wanted his son to study medicine. Now, almost unthinkingly, his son revealed his secret: the intelligence of the body.

Felix was moved. His son was no wild oaf but a boy with his own virtues. A sound body will always reduce the complexities of life to the proper simplicity. He would not be a physician or an attorney, but a man among men. He had chosen well. What kind of faces did those lawyers have as they scurried up the courthouse stairs, thin, pale, and nasty because of their great physical weakness?

"Where did you learn to bowl?"

"I didn't learn." Karl purposely spoke with nonchalance.

"How's that?"

"You don't learn those games. Only fools are taught to ride, to throw a ball, or row a boat. There's no need to learn."

Now he understood something he hadn't grasped all those years: the private tutors who used to visit the house every day, it was they who had muddied his spirit, along with his Jewish friends who had sought to excel at any price. "You should play a lot of sports." Felix spoke without knowing what he was saying.

"I agree." Karl confirmed his words. "Were you good at sports?"

"No, to my regret." Felix tried to shake off the question lightly.

"Why not?"

"I don't know."

"At your school did they have regular physical education classes?"

"They did, but I wasn't good in them."

"Why not?"

"In my day physical education classes weren't considered important."

"Didn't they used to say, 'A sound mind in a sound body'?"

"They said it," Felix replied, and a smile settled on his lips as though he had been caught in a minor transgression. Now he remembered his classmates, gentile and sturdy, who used to fill the gymnasium with clouds of sweat. In mathematics and Latin they did poorly. They would stand at the blackboard as though rebuked, but on the playing field they excited both teachers and pupils. Frequently their fathers would appear, landlords and factory owners, interceding in their sons' behalf. For the school was a prestigious one. The three Jews had suffered more than a little on account of their short stature and academic prowess.

They sat in the buffet and drank coffee. The cloudy skies gradually cleared, and the sunlight, moist and perfumed, spread out at their feet. Felix was pleased that his distant son, whom he had taken to be a mindless dolt for years, had ultimately turned out to be a creature with true achievements.

"I wasn't any good at sports, and it's too bad I wasn't." Felix returned to the conversation. "A graceful body is a healthy one, isn't that right? Now, at my age, it's too late."

"You could still repair the damage."

"I don't believe so."

"It's a question of will." Karl spoke definitely, the way they speak in the army.

"Perhaps the will exists, but there isn't much ability." Felix tried to defend himself.

"If a person wishes, he can."

Felix imagined he heard the voice of a master sergeant in that statement, one who not only gives orders but also arranges his trainees' lives. He chuckled, and Karl, who did not understand the significance of that laugh, went back and took up his theme again: "If a person wishes, he can."

"You're right, son." Felix made a gesture toward him, somewhat to appease the boy. For years he had been persecuted by bad teachers who demanded the impossible of him.

When they returned to the inn at noon, Henrietta and Helga were sitting in the brightly lit foyer. A prayerbook lay open on the table. A thick, mountain tranquility rested upon the blue vases which stood polished along the windows. "What are you doing?" Felix asked in his ordinary voice.

"Nothing." Henrietta blushed.

Helga opened her eyes wide, and frightening wonderment shook her gaze. "We are learning the Hebrew letters."

"And you find that interesting?"

Felix was angry at Henrietta, at her way of sitting, at the kerchief she had bound around her head. Her thin features, which not many years ago had charmed his eyes, now seemed thick to him, ambitious, with but a single intention: to impose her mastery on Helga.

"Helga," he wanted to call within himself, "come back to yourself, remove the bonds, don't be drawn into superstition." His love for Helga, the hidden, disappointed love of a father, stirred inside him. His hands shook with the strength of the emotion. He closed his eyes without saying a word and turned away.

"What's that?" Karl asked Helga.

"A Jewish prayerbook, haven't you seen one?"

"Not from up close," Karl said, and his full face, reddened with the cold, shrank, as though he had been served some tasteless food. "Who's reading it?"

"We are," Henrietta intervened. She looked at his full face for a moment, from a distance, as though he weren't her son whom she had nursed, and whose golden curls, at the age of two, had been pleasant to touch. She trembled at that feeling of distance and, greatly discouraged, she said: "We are learning to pray."

"Who needs that?" His response was not delayed.

Of course Karl didn't grasp the complexity, and it was also hard to explain to him. Henrietta grimaced strangely and turned to him, in a tone that sounded imploring. "We want to appeal to God, so that He, in His great mercy, will have pity on us."

Karl took the prayerbook in his hands, looked at the large letters, leafed through it, and said: "It's hard for me to understand what anyone finds in this scribbling."

Henrietta opened her eyes. For a moment she was

53

going to reprimand him, but seeing his face, an awkward face, yet not a mean one, she kept still. Helga, seeing her mother's discomfiture said: "Those are Hebrew letters. Mother learned them in her childhood. From her mother. And now she's teaching me."

"What do you need that for?" he asked gruffly.

"For prayer."

"What? To pray?" He had finally caught his sister, known for her fine intelligence and many talents, talking nonsense. Strangely Helga did not argue her case. She looked at him softly and forgivingly, the look of an older sister who no longer can be insulted by her young brother.

VI

THEN CAME icy cold days, and Felix would sit on the veranda during most of the daylight hours and stare out at the back courtyard. In the afternoon the blue light would filter through the woods and spread out at the foot of the fence. His distant, extensive business dealings were gradually erased from his mind. Occasionally the factory managers would penetrate the curtain of distance. Strangely Felix suspected no one, not even his closest assistant, a notorious skirt-chaser and gambler.

"I'm going back soon," he would say. But it was clear that he would not be descending in the near future.

Henrietta, in contrast, was busy and frighteningly practical. For hours she would sit and study with Helga. Helga was diligent, and within a week she could already read "Hear, O Israel" from the prayerbook. An alien look of satisfaction filled Henrietta's face. Her forehead was cold and monastic, a look that aroused disgust in Felix's heart.

Later Henrietta said: "We are going to see the healer. Wouldn't you like to join us?"

"I prefer to remain here. I am comfortable here." For some reason he spoke redundantly. Henrietta put on her brown dress, which buttoned up the neck. The dress gave a kind of sturdiness to her figure, perhaps because it made her shoulders stand out. Felix was frightened by the thought that within a short time Helga would once again be standing at the entrance of that neglected house, surrounded by poor people, near the attendant whose entire energies were bent on gain. "Don't go!" he wanted to call out angrily, though he knew that his outcry would not hold them back. They would go even if it hailed. In a short while they were standing in the courtyard, wrapped in winter coats, on their way to the forest. Helga, noticing him, called out, "Adieu, Father," and they disappeared.

From there he could observe Karl bowling. His shots were strong and accurate, never missing. He did not speak much with the peasants, but they followed his movements politely. He sent the ball nicely, without visible effort. That hidden Karl had been unknown to him. Now that he had been revealed, Felix took pleasure in him. For a moment he thought of getting up and approaching his son, but he thought better of it. He did not wish to embarrass him. A short, bald man is nothing to be proud of.

When they returned from the healer's dwelling it was already dark. Felix saw them from a distance. They walked arm in arm. From the foyer window they seemed shorter than usual. That, of course, was an illusion. They were happy and pleased with themselves, and that angered him.

"How was it?" He greeted them with an expression of equanimity.

"Good," said Henrietta. "The healer was satisfied. I might say quite satisfied."

"With what?"

"With Helga's progress in learning the prayers."

"Will it do her any good?"

Henrietta did not reply. Her look, which had first been broad and content, constricted all at once.

Felix rose, and with words which had been stored up in him for many hours, addressed Henrietta. "Tell me, what good will it do—just annoy me?"

Henrietta stood for a moment, stunned. She grasped Helga's arm and together they went upstairs. Felix remained where he was. The evening lights, filtering into the foyer, were completely blue. Some old strength, which he had not known for years, gripped him for a moment, and the words he had suppressed burst out powerfully as a curse: "The devil take her, the devil take her," as though Henrietta had not returned from the healer, but from Dr. Rufhaus, a gynecologist notorious for shamelessly fornicating with his patients.

Meanwhile Karl had entered, heavy and sweaty. He had squeezed the last drop out of the day. Now he seemed like a laborer after work, hungry and weary.

"What's there to eat?" He threw the words out like a peasant.

The innkeeper's wife, who had heard his voice, said in motherly tones: "Sit down, I'll make you a sandwich. Wash your hands in the meantime."

In a moment or two Karl was sitting at the low table in the corner of the dining room. His face, which was washed, seemed disheveled and blurry. He took big bites of his sandwich. His entire being bespoke ravenous hunger.

"The stranger woman is serving him food. She knows the boy's needs better than his mother," the thought flashed through Felix's mind. "His mother's head is full of nonsense." For a moment he thought of stepping out of the darkness and approaching his son, but his son beat him to it and walked over to him.

"Father?"

"What, my dear."

"I beat them again."

"How?" Felix tried to draw him out. Clearly the quiet pleasure that filled his son's muscular body had no need of words. Felix, for his part, was pleased that he hadn't asked about his mother, and that small pleasure sweetened his contact with him.

Later Henrietta and Helga came downstairs dressed for dinner, with hair combed and neat. Felix followed their slow progress intently. He could tell they had drawn closer to each other since their arrival, in dress and now even in hairstyle: Helga's hair was now cut short.

"Let's eat," Henrietta said out loud, as though they were not in a strange place, but at home.

"I'm not hungry," Felix answered from his place in the foyer.

"Daddy." Helga spoke in an artificial voice. "Won't you join us?"

Felix did not respond. From a distance he saw them taking their places at the table. Helga's opaque face had opened somewhat, and a smile which had not been seen there for months rose and blossomed. Karl went for the food without ceremony.

Felix sat frozen and bound. The thought that his beloved daughter was content in Henrietta's company, that thought kindled some old rage, and he rose to his feet and went outside.

The night was bright and humid, windless. Now, as on the day of their arrival, he noted how low the houses were next to the mighty trees. The sounds rising from the valley were clear and light. "Pretty," he said, and began walking. For a long time he walked without looking, immersed in himself, without thoughts. Abruptly he stopped next to a lighted window. A table lamp, a woman sitting and reading. Strange, that tranquil sight suddenly set him trembling with fatigue. He felt like collapsing and falling asleep. The struggle with Henrietta had become too heavy to bear. Her self-assurance had always been greater than his, but that night, as she came downstairs in her brown dress, she seemed firmer than ever in her opinion. Her carriage bespoke arrogance. It occurred to him that she had tried to dominate the children all those years. Now she had found the way.

Then he found himself near a stream and tried in vain to drive those thoughts from him. While he was standing there, a powerful desire gripped him: for a cup of coffee. He immediately turned his back on the bright sights of the night and returned, following his own tracks. As he progressed, the desire took hold of him ever more strongly. He was certain that if a cup of coffee and a pack of cigarettes were placed before him, the nightmare would pass, and a life with light and repose would be restored to him.

The inn was dark. A single servant, a tall, strong woman, stood in the kitchen, kneading dough. "Coffee," he called out. Miraculously the servant understood and served him a cup of coffee on a tray with a pack of cigarettes. Her smile was one of obedience and devotion. For a moment he thought of hugging her and kissing her neck, but seeing her hands, strong hands, red and moist, he was deterred and sat on the bench. He sat and drank the coffee, and with every sip his spirit returned to him. His eyes were opened. Suddenly he remembered Helga's artificial voice, and the memory dampened his spirit.

VII

THE DAYS WERE GLOOMY and rainy, and Felix sat on the veranda for hours without exchanging a word with anyone. An alien feeling spread over his body like a skin disease. In the empty dining room Henrietta and Helga would sit for hours, repeating the prayers out loud. More than once he felt like getting up and silencing them. He didn't have any strength in his legs. He was imprisoned in himself as though in a space with no exit. But, in contrast, he would argue for hours with the innkeeper, a moderate man with a closed look, who had spent his youth in Vienna. Now, it seemed, nothing remained of the man's urbanity. He spoke faulty German mixed with words in Ruthenian. Felix constantly tried to convince him that a man's place was in the city. Religion had completely died out. One should no longer heed old writings. Not everything written in holy letters was stamped with the seal of sanctity. There were many fakers and tricksters.

The man listened but was in no hurry to answer. Since he didn't answer, Felix inundated him with words upon words, set against him, trying to make him admit that most of the healers called rebbes were mere fakes. The man listened very attentively but without responding.

That muteness drove Felix out of his mind. "Haven't you any opinion? You're a local." Felix addressed him imperiously. "You know the secrets, the humbugs. Can't you help me, confirm my feeling? I'm not asking for anything but the plain truth." Not even that direct appeal would dislodge the man from his muteness. He pursed his lips, clenched his fists, and did not answer. Since he did not answer, Felix returned to his place, the wicker chair in the foyer.

From there he planned his return home. The return to Vienna filled his being to the brim. If only he could slip away that very night. A few days of distance attached him powerfully to his native city. He was like a drunkard who is denied alcohol. For the moment the chances of returning were slender. Heavy rains slashed down unremittingly. The roads were impassable. Every hour a boulder tumbled out of its place or a tree fell. The water in the streambeds roared deafeningly. But indoors it was hot. The dry logs crackled lightly in the fire. A pleasant warmth with a piney smell spread through the rooms, but that pleasure couldn't soothe his sadness. Now it was clear to him: separation was at hand. Better to bring the time nearer. Helga, since her hair had been cut, looked like Henrietta—even the way she held her neck. From time to time she would say, "No matter," emphatically, as only Henrietta pronounced that phrase.

The innkeeper's wife rose early and prepared the baking oven. Darkness and the flicker of the lamps brought to mind an old ceremony. After prayers she would serve fresh rolls tasting of the oven's coals. Every morning a quorum would gather for prayers. The first days he had not heard the prayers. Now they woke him and crumbled his sleep to bits. Even the rains could not damp those low tones, climbing softly up to the bedrooms.

Therefore he rose early, sitting in the foyer and waiting for breakfast. The innkeeper's wife tried to appease him with hot coffee, a roll, and her homemade jam. But it did not help. The sadness oppressed him. The more he sat and looked at the people sitting beside him and eating their fill, the greater his irritation became. They were mostly Jews passing through, whose wagons full of merchandise awaited them in the courtyard. In a short while they would ride to distant, isolated villages to sell their goods to the peasants. For the moment they were sitting at ease and eating. The innkeeper's wife did not stint on food, serving them the best she had. The innkeeper also did his utmost so that the guests would be content. Felix tried to absorb their language, but in vain. He understood not a single word. Meanwhile a few pure rays of light filtered through the thick, heavy clouds, illuminating the merchants' faces. Before much time passed, they were bundled up in their thick coats, hastily saying grace, and paying the innkeeper with colorful bank notes.

Felix did not budge from his place. From nearby he heard the creaking of the wheels, the neighing of the horses, and the whips cracking. The wagons jerked into motion, leaving the stillness of the morning intact.

For a long time Felix sat in his place, lighting one cigarette with another. The smoke calmed his raw nerves somewhat, and his eyes closed for a moment.

When Henrietta and Helga came downstairs, light was already spread in every corner of the dining room. There was no sign that about ten merchants had lain there the previous night. The rustic carpets were clean and a strong, sheepy odor of wool wafted up from them. Henrietta turned her face up and called out a greeting, "Good morning." The innkeeper's wife came to Felix's assistance, announcing, "Your husband has already been awake for hours. He has eaten and drunk."

That announcement did not ease Henrietta's discomposure. She sat erect in her place, Helga at her side, and placed a napkin on her lap. "How are you? Why did you get up early?" Henrietta asked.

That simple question annoyed Felix very much, and he said, "I constantly think of how I can leave this place. How long can one sit here without doing anything?"

"How can you depart in this rain, in this frost?" As it left her mouth, the question was as cold as ice.

"It's not so terrible, not so terrible." Felix tried to shrug off her opinion.

But Henrietta insisted: "I don't know what to say to you."

"I wasn't asking for advice." Felix lashed her with his words.

"Father, why do you want to leave us?" Helga surprised him with her clear voice.

"Who will watch over the business, the house? Can I leave everything in the clerks' hands?"

Henrietta drank her coffee. With all her senses she absorbed that tone, familiar to her for years. An involuntary smile spread on her lips. Helga stubbornly added fat to the fire: "Don't leave." Those words were entirely external. That mere outwardness, from his daughter, was hardest of all for him to bear.

"Do as you wish. Anyway you won't listen to me," said Henrietta in a merciless voice.

"Don't worry," Felix replied, irrelevantly.

Immediately afterward Karl came downstairs and sat in his place. His face was rumpled and confused with slumber. Ugly pink pimples spread over it. "Doubtless he has already been in a whorehouse." A strange smile rose on Felix's lips. "Is there any way of stopping him?" However, to tell the truth, it wasn't that corruption which annoyed him, but rather the shape of the boy's face. In the morning his face was like his mother's, even the tension in the corners of his lips, his ears.

Afterward Helga took her mother's arm and they went up to the bedroom. Karl lingered for a long time, dipping bread in sour cream, and you could see his appetite was boundless. Felix wanted to say a word to his son, but he could not find even a single one within him. The silence between them oppressed him.

It was around nine o'clock, and the morning sights passed before Felix's eyes one by one: the merchants standing at prayer, eating their fill, and saying grace. There was some power, he had to admit, in their solidarity as they sat. Now they were already scattered among the low, thatched huts, from which the odor of fresh milk and moist straw rose in the chilly morning hours.

He relished the rolls and coffee which the innkeeper's wife had served him. For a long time he had sat in the corner, observing the merchants as they sat solidly together, without understanding a word. Afterward he noticed: a certain earnestness marked their faces, that of men who do their duty without complaint.

Now he knew with simple clarity that Karl too would turn his back on him some day. The offspring were bound like cubs to their mother who had borne them. In the end fathers were forgotten. Felix sought to sweeten his sorrow with that strange generalization.

"Father."

"What?" Felix was startled.

"I need a little money."

Felix took two bills out of his jacket pocket and handed them to his son. Karl took them without thanking him. Felix was glad his son had included him in his secret deeds.

VIII

BETWEEN ONE MEAL and another, Felix asked
about the train schedule, horses, and wagons. It was
clear to everyone, the heights were cut off; no one could
come or go. The merchants and peddlers weren't concerned. For a long time they had looked forward to that
season, which would free them of their worries. Now
they were relaxed, burdened with actions and dozing
on low couches.

In the afternoon Felix wrapped himself in his coat
and went out to the dairy. There were few people at the
buffet. The owner, a short, opinionated Jew, served him
coffee and preached him an old sermon: "Time is not
on our side. Every day brings a new evil."

His voice was not pleasant, and Felix had inci-
sive words to rebut his assertions, but made no reply.

"How does one get to the railway?" That was his only question.

"The streams are swollen, the roads are flooded. Can't you see with your own eyes?"

He had been getting that answer for days. It made him burn with rage.

Nevertheless he was in no hurry to return to the inn. For a long time he sat and looked at the few people sitting there trading impressions and joking. Jews of a new sort, not religious, wandering between city and town, stopping over here.

The owner of the buffet, it appeared, was not an easygoing person. He rebuked them for their frivolity, for wasting money on women, for forgetting to return home. Strangely, the peddlers did not get angry at him. "You're right," they would say, "you're right in every respect. It's good you reprimand us. You'll be well rewarded in the next world." Even though the proprietor knew those wags were not serious, he was appeased, serving them cups of pungent coffee, preparing sandwiches for them, no longer scolding them for the vulgar innuendos they made to each other.

The sky grew darker, and the southern frost took ever-stronger possession of the back courtyard. Helga was prone to oppressive, ever-changing moods. Henrietta would shelter her, saying, "The girl is weary. She needs to rest." Henrietta's face grew more and more haggard, and her brow broadened. She was aggressively opinionated as new believers tend to be. Quick motions without pleasure. Without noticing it, Felix too had become ensnared in threads of gloom and fear.

But with him it was different: to rescue Helga from her mother, to flee with her before nightfall. Clearly those were hallucinations.

Helga clung to her mother like a little girl. She would not move unless summoned by her voice. In moments of darkness she would cry out: "Mommy, save me, I'm drowning." Now Felix was tensely living the swell and ebb of his sick daughter.

One evening Helga surprised him by approaching him and asking: "Father, why are you sad?"

"It's nothing, just a mood." He was startled out of his seat and rose to his feet.

The old, moderate expression returned to her face. It seemed she was about to say a sentence about Professor Poldak, her music teacher, something like, "Nevertheless, on second thought," something like, "Yet he does have something to say about music." For a moment she observed her father quietly and whispered, "Why don't we go out for a walk?"

"Certainly." However, immediately a strange embarrassment seized him, and he said, "But the rain. Isn't it raining?"

"The rain has stopped." Helga spoke in a clear voice.

Noiselessly they slipped away into the nearby woods. The evening light shone on them and wrapped them in its cloak. For a long while they walked in the cold moisture without exchanging a word. The secret of past days sheltered their way.

And Felix, who was crammed with words, did not know what to say. After they had gone some distance he found, at last, some words and said: "How are you?"

Helga, who understood his embarrassment, took his arm, a sign of affection from old times. She said, "I am in excellent health. I'm concerned about you. You're tired, aren't you?"

"Somewhat."

"Are you worried?"

"Somewhat."

"Am I worrying you?"

"No," he lied.

Helga raised the collar of her coat, grasping its lapels and covering the nape of her neck. A smile returned to her face, a smile with a hint of cunning, as though she had caught her father doing something wrong. Oddly, Felix felt a bit relieved.

He then spoke loudly and hurriedly. He admitted he hadn't done well to agree to come here to this isolated place where the people were obtuse. It was no coincidence they inclined toward superstition. Now he would make every effort to go back down. There was no sense staying. In his haste, the words thinned out in his mouth, and he repeated himself. When he realized he was repeating himself, he stopped and asked Helga, "Why didn't you interrupt me?"

"I like to hear your voice, Daddy," she answered simply.

Many feelings pent up within him sought to break out, but words stood in his way, as though they were lost to him. He stood beside his daughter, perplexed. "We're going back, we're going back soon, we're wasting time," he muttered.

"Father, wouldn't it be a good idea to rest for a few days?"

"Not here, by no means. I must return to the factory, and you have no piano. Here you can't practice."

"True, I miss that," she admitted.

"Of course you miss that."

They did not speak of Henrietta. Only once Helga said, "Wouldn't it be a good idea to ask Mother?" But she immediately took it back. The evening light spread out across the horizon, red and blue. As it continued, it grew more brilliant. Helga, who had been sensitive to light since her childhood, said: "Come, Father. Let's cross over into the shade."

They turned and walked in the shadow of the tall trees, and Helga spoke with quiet incisiveness and in tones devoid of excess, of the need to find a different teacher. A teacher with a bright, roomy studio, not like Poldak, whose studio was dark and smelled moldy even in the summer. Felix agreed with her and also admitted that, though Poldak was well known, his behavior was far from attractive. It would be best to find a new teacher soon.

The evening darkened and they walked along the path, wrapped in the old words and in odors that had come alive again. Felix's excitement swelled and, greatly moved, he did not notice that Helga spoke fewer and fewer words, and those which she did utter were as heavy as stones.

Since she was not speaking, he spoke of the urgent need to return home soon—he to his factory and she to the piano. The piano was a great instrument, in which many secrets were still concealed, and they had to be brought out into the light of the world. It was unfortunate that his father had been a poor man and could not afford to hire a music teacher. A man without music is flawed. Something of his enthusiasm infected Helga, apparently. She walked after him, taking long strides as though trying to overtake him.

While he was cleaving the darkness with long steps, deluging her with words, entirely possessed with a single desire—to restore Helga to the piano—she burst out laughing. Her laughter was full and loud. Apparently she had remembered Poldak or his assistant. Felix continued talking, and as he continued, he knew that it had not been laughter but rather the evil voice which had possessed her and was torturing her. His legs trembled, and he stopped. "We know that Poldak is a sadist, a base person. There are other teachers, good and pleasant ones, modest men who can appreciate a pure tone." He spoke moderately, but with strength, trying to bind the wound with gentleness.

It was late. Helga's voice was now completely broken. Strange, throttled noises emerged from her throat. But between one choking sound and another she spoke of the need to return to the piano once and for all, and to a well-planned daily schedule: scales, études, and pieces; not to lose a single day, to attend lectures at the conservatory, also to join a chorus. Felix knew that it was not her voice but rather that evil voice which had attached itself to her. What frightened him was its earnestness.

From the tall trees flakes of thick darkness fell, spreading silently next to the trunks. Felix now saw that slow descent clearly, and how they spread their thin wings. Not a sound was heard, only Helga's tremulous voice. "Soon we'll find the way," he murmured. His feet expressed his fear more than his arms.

Before much time passed, to his horror he discovered Henrietta. She was standing at the side, in the shadows, her figure tensed like an animal.

"Get away from here!" Felix shouted loudly. Henrietta bent but did not move. There was no way out of that dark thicket—only face-to-face.

"What are you doing here?" He addressed Henrietta as one addresses a servant woman who is found where she does not belong.

"I went out for a walk." The words trembled in her mouth.

"You were lying in wait for us." He could not restrain his voice.

"I came out to look for you." Henrietta defended herself.

Felix raised his hands for some reason. That movement frightened Helga, and she burst into tears. Henrietta hushed her and hugged her. "It's nothing, child, nothing." For a moment he stood and watched the women hugging each other. The fury spilled out of his hands, his muscles went slack, lassitude gripped his legs. But he overcame it and climbed up the slope. The front wing of the inn was lit. The one behind it was in darkness, the windows sealed.

IX

IN DECEMBER it snowed without letup. In the evenings the sky would turn blue with a cold burnish, recalling broad expanses of new metal. Felix would sit in the foyer for hours. The anger which had seethed in him now stopped tormenting him. Only Henrietta's steps would fill him with fear. Henrietta had changed beyond recognition. She was thinner, stooped, and the kerchief on her head gave her the look of a sister in a Catholic hospital. The sadness that had filled her face since the beginning of Helga's illness had also changed. It was an unfeeling sadness. She did not remove her front-laced high shoes, and her entire being bespoke firmness. Helga heeded her discipline wordlessly.

"I'm going back soon," Felix announced.

Henrietta was not surprised. Naked practicality now peered forth from her silent eyes.

"At the first opportunity," he announced again.

"It's cold. Everything is frozen. How will you leave?" the words left Henrietta's mouth.

What had been hidden for several years was now suddenly stripped bare. Words no longer hid the bitter truth: separation was inevitable.

While the winter light spread, growing stronger, Helga disappeared. Karl was the first to notice her absence. Felix apparently did not grasp the seriousness of the situation, since he went outside and returned, announcing, "Snow is everywhere. There's not a single sign of life." The innkeeper's wife and the servant women were more alert. They put on boots, wrapped themselves in heavy winter coats, and went outside, standing at the edge of the slope.

"What shall I shout out?" asked the cook.

"Shout 'Helga,' " answered the innkeeper's wife.

She proved to have a strong voice, spreading far and wide and sounding like a wild moan.

Henrietta had come out meanwhile, also wearing boots, and without asking anyone, she headed straight for the slope.

"Where are you going?" One of the maids stopped her.

"To search for my daughter. Does it make any sense to stand here?" A strange smile covered her face, as though she knew what to do in times of trouble such as this.

"It's very dangerous. The slope is steep," the maid said.

"She's mad. Let her go." Felix did not curb his voice.

Hearing that remark, Henrietta stood still. The strange smile did not fade from her face. Her eyes glowed with a strong light.

"Shout again," the innkeeper's wife said to the cook.

"What shall I shout?" asked the servant in a raw voice.

"I told you. Shout 'Helga.' "

The cook, making an effort to do her employer's will, emitted a whinny that set the air around her trembling. In the meantime the innkeeper had harnessed the horse to his little sleigh and started on his way.

"Take me along," Felix said to him in a soft, friendly voice.

"Gladly," said the innkeeper. "But this sled isn't comfortable."

"That doesn't matter." Felix spoke as though in the grip of a dream and jumped onto the sleigh.

They left, and the sky began to shower thick snowflakes. The cook, standing at the top of the slope, shouted again. Her voice, the voice of a frightened beast, was swallowed up in the thick swirls of snow. Henrietta now stood among the servant women, her stiff face became even stiffer.

"Where has the girl been?" the innkeeper's wife wanted to know.

"She was with me, with me," Henrietta hurriedly answered, pleased that, finally, they were addressing her.

"And when did she go out?"

"I fell asleep. Apparently I fell asleep." She rushed to accuse herself. "But, great God, how could she disappear here?"

The maids half-smiled. They knew: nothing was easier than to disappear in that barren place.

"We'll yet find her alive," she said imploringly to the maids in Germanized Yiddish.

"We'll find her, no doubt about it," they answered as one woman. Strangely that fortuitous promise had its effect. The frozen smile on her face softened, as though a hidden hand had stroked her.

"Apparently I fell asleep," she said again. "I didn't imagine anyone would go out in this cold."

"Didn't she say anything?" inquired the innkeeper's wife. Her look was broad and penetrating.

"Nothing, by my faith, nothing."

"Strange."

"This snow draws people as though with cords," one of the maids said in Ruthenian mixed with German words.

"God, help me," Henrietta burst out loud, as if she had just now grasped the disaster.

"He will help. He will help. He always helps." The maid comforted her in an unconvincing tone of voice. Her face, wrapped in a thick peasant scarf, showed that she knew how to take care of herself in any trouble.

The snow fell harder. Henrietta stood still without uttering a word. The servant women shouted, waving pitchforks and spades, ancient signs of trouble and distress.

"How long has the girl been sick?" abruptly asked one of the old servant women who had not joined in the shouting.

"She isn't sick, just moody," Henrietta said, retreating somewhat, away from the direct words that had been cast at her. But seeing the peasant woman's look, a straightforward, sturdy look which sought only the real truth, she took back what she said. "Her illness isn't as severe as it might look. The past two years haven't been easy for her."

"God will help her, God is the only savior," the peasant woman said piously.

"Thank you" emerged from Henrietta's lips.

"Not to us is thanks due but to God on high." She rebuked her somewhat.

"Certainly." She tried to correct herself.

The peasant woman raised her head and in a voice which made the entire place shudder, she joined the chorus of shouting women: "Come out, girl, come out." Henrietta bent over as though it were not a woman's voice but thunder rushing down from above.

Before an hour passed the sleigh returned without any good tidings. In fact, they had not gone far. Felix descended from the sleigh with an agile movement, as though he had not returned from a desperate search but from a business trip, which included a bit of pleasure. "How're things?" he asked the servant women, ignoring Henrietta's presence completely.

"There's nothing," said the cook.

"We must fortify ourselves with patience." Felix

spoke as he might to the good-natured owner of a
factory when one of his machines stopped working.
Henrietta opened her mouth as though the husband
familiar to her had not spoken but rather a stranger
whose voice was alien.

"Didn't you see any footprints?" the cook asked again.

"No," he said, and a smile split his face. The innkeeper's wife spoke to the women now, waving her
hands. Finally all the women stood together at the edge
of the slope, and in unison they shouted: "Helga,
Helga, come out of the snow." A vestige of an ancient
rite, when one's hand has lost its power to help.

Karl left the scene and secretly entered the tavern.
From that corner he could be seen in profile, throwing
darts at the target. Felix, who noticed him, was not
angry at him. He was angry at Henrietta, at her boots,
at the way she was standing, which bespoke awkward
numbness. The snow fell harder. The servant women
turned their backs to the slope, moving as quickly as
their heavy boots permitted them, taking shelter.

"What shall we do?" the innkeeper's wife said, cracking her knuckles.

"We must wait and see." Felix spoke in a voice not his
own. Even now he had not grasped the full extent of
the disaster. His long face expressed a kind of strange
equanimity.

"She'll come back yet," one of the clumsy servant
women said, the way, in a village, one speaks about
miracles which are long in coming. In the meantime
the cloudy sky grew darker.

Henrietta, standing at the side all the while, gripped by muteness, took several steps forward and said: "Apparently I fell asleep. How could I not have stopped her? Stopped myself? I don't understand."

"It happens," one of the servant women comforted her insincerely.

"You mustn't fall asleep when there's a girl at home, you mustn't," she tortured herself in a whisper.

Felix, who had heard the reprimand, put on a serious face and spoke with a loud, arrogant voice. "Why did you bring her here?"

Henrietta, who had not apparently expected him to mix in, froze in her place. Now it seemed as though in a moment she would fall prostrate onto the snow. She spread her arms as though to lean on something. That movement helped her, apparently, for she did not fall.

"No one told you to bring her here," he harried her. Now it seemed as though she was going to make some reply, but that was an illusion. Her pursed lips were sealed.

The innkeeper's wife sensed the flames about to flare up, and in a motherly voice she spoke out. "Let's go inside. It's dark already."

"I'm not going in," Henrietta announced, half fearful, half obstinate.

"Leave her. You can't argue with her," said Felix, and without delay he went inside. For a moment they all stood in the entrance, covered by the snow that had clung to their clothing. The servant women broke the silence and began treading with their heavy feet. The rustic carpet was covered with a layer of trampled snow. Before long the women were in the kitchen, preparing supper.

Felix stood completely still, beside the pane in the door. All his anger was now directed at his wife, who was standing outside. For a moment he felt like opening the window and shouting a vulgar word. The anger simmering inside him paralyzed him. And, as after every disaster, his knees went weak.

At dinner salted fish was served, with sour cream and cheese. The fish were fresh and tasty, and Felix ate two portions. Karl, sitting across from him, ate distractedly.

"Will we go out looking for her tonight?" Karl asked his father.

"I don't know. Why are you asking me?"

"I'd join in."

"I have no horses, no lanterns. I have nothing."

"I just wanted to know," Karl apologized.

"What good would it do?" Felix poured his anger out on him too.

After supper the people scattered, and Felix sat on the narrow sofa in the corner of the veranda for a long time. After about an hour he fell asleep, and Karl went outside to his mother. She refused to come in. She sat motionless with her legs crossed. The snow stopped, and the frost was bitter. Since his pleas were useless, the innkeeper's wife and the servant women came to his assistance. They swore they would not let her freeze. Finally, having no alternative, they dragged her in with entreaties. In the entrance she ceased resisting. Her face was red and blurry. The servant women gave her a cup of hot coffee, and Henrietta grasped the vessel with both hands. After drinking she felt better, apparently, for she fell asleep. One of the servant women placed a pillow under her head. A feeling of relief descended upon them all, as though they had done their duty.

But the innkeeper did not rest. He recruited a few villagers, and they went out to the mountains. All night long their sleighs combed the snow-covered hills. Toward morning snow began falling again. The peasants were tired and the dogs raced about angrily. The innkeeper could no longer detain them. "The Lord has given, and the Lord has taken away," a peasant declared, giving the sign to return home. Close to the village, next to a thick tree trunk, they saw a person's body. The peasants didn't ask "Who are you, what are you doing here?" They hefted her onto the sleigh and set out. Before long the good news spread like fire.

Strange, Henrietta was the one they had to rouse. When she woke up she asked, "What do you want from me?"

"She's alive," one of the servant women shouted deafeningly. Immediately many firm hands spread out upon Helga and massaged her to warm her frozen limbs. Helga's face expressed a kind of opaque awkwardness. As the massage grew stronger, her lips twisted with pain. Felix stood at her side without taking his eyes off her. He knew that a miracle had taken place for him that night. He wanted to be happy, to get drunk and give clothing to the servant women, but he could not overcome the fear that bathed his body in sweat. He trembled.

Henrietta crawled to the hearth on her knees. When she saw Helga, she broke out in a strange wail: "I told you, you didn't believe me." The servant women stepped aside, and she put her hand on Helga's brow. "Give me some brandy," she ordered.

Felix turned his back and sat down, as at the beginning of the evening, on the narrow sofa. In vain he sought to calm the tremors in his body.

X

THE NEXT DAY Henrietta sat on Helga's bed and fed her applesauce with a spoon. The winter light filled the windows, the heated rooms, and were it not for the dread remaining in him, Felix would have put on boots and gone out to take a look around. From his youth he had liked the snow. Before long he overcame his dread, and with steps which had a kind of determination to them, he went outside. For some reason it was important to him to be outside, near that very tree trunk upon which Helga had leaned her head.

The sky was open, blue, and unspotted. The sun spread its light upon the white glow and emitted dry cold. Felix was bundled up from head to foot, and his desire to march was stronger than his fatigue. He was certain that if he strode straight ahead, without turning aside, he would quickly reach that tree trunk. He imagined he saw the place clearly, therefore he feared neither man nor the beast of the field. On the contrary, old strength which had been hidden in him for years returned and flooded his muscles, and as he advanced, he felt that his legs were bearing him well.

A kind of distant and forgotten joy surrounded him on all sides, and he was within himself, but not walled off. If he had met someone, he would have told of some inconsequential things which had given him happiness over the years. He wanted to laugh the way boys and girls laugh when they're together. "True, I was not a good athlete, but I always loved to hike," he said to himself. For a long time he walked without pausing. A fresh power drew him forward, and he advanced.

At about three o'clock he sat down. The fatigue of the previous night now lurked in all his bones, but he knew that one must not lean one's head on a tree trunk. One's head must remain erect. A few jets of cold filtered through his thick clothing. That did not slow his steps. His body was warm, at the correct temperature.

The light was full, and he advanced. Distant sights from his gymnasium years stood before his eyes with great freshness. Those had not been easy times. The competition was stiff, particularly for the Jews. They leaped ahead. Two were actually geniuses. He made great efforts, not always succeeding. But what good would it have done had he succeeded? His father could not afford to send him to the university. As he sank deeper into those visions, he heard the mooing of a distant cow. He roused himself and looked about him: "I won't let events dominate me. A man's fate is in his own hands." These were old words, spoken from his throat with an alien assurance.

A vision of the morning returned to him with an exposed chilliness. Helga was lying supine on two immaculate pillows and Henrietta was feeding her applesauce. For a long time he had stood at the threshold and watched. It had seemed to him that Helga was trying to rise and get out of bed, that the food was repugnant to her, but Henrietta had blockaded her, sitting on her bed and restraining her. "Let her get up," he had wanted to shout, but his throat was obstructed.

Now it was clear to him: if he should reach that tree trunk upon which Helga had laid her head, he would free her from bondage. That assurance strengthened his legs all at once. He was certain that the way was not long now, and if he made an effort, he would reach it before dark.

Evening fell. The tall birches rose over the snow-drifts, tall and solid, as though they were not trees but wooden beams which someone had stuck into the ground at random and would gather up in the dark. Felix stood and observed them closely. The thin shadows intertwined to form quivering squares, which stretched into narrow oblongs from moment to moment.

Now some random visions flitted before his eyes. They passed before him slowly, with soft steps. He did not remember all the faces, nor did he know all the details, but when they drew near him, they looked upon him graciously. "It isn't so terrible here," he said, not knowing what he was talking about.

Darkness fell and he was unafraid. For a moment he wished to kneel down and doze off. He knew that would be a grave dereliction. He had to advance at any cost. Hardly had he made up his mind, when his head sank and touched the tree trunk. A pleasant feeling spread the length of his body, and his fall reminded him, as though by magic, of another winter, a heated room, and he was lying on thick cushions, with a package of Swiss chocolate on the bureau, an irresponsible sprawl. The sight from former times stuck to his eyelids for a moment and was interred. Only a hovering feeling remained, flowing blindly along his buried body.

Several times he tried to rouse himself and stand up. He knew that his legs were not tied, but the bonds of sleep were stronger than his willpower, and he remained glued to the earth. Now the pleasant feeling streamed in the direction of his knees, to the regions of his back and shoulders. For some reason his neck either did not absorb or refused to absorb that pleasure. He knew that he must not lie down, that it was a sin for which there was no repenting, but, as in a nightmare, he was bound. When he tried to rouse himself he felt it was beyond his power.

Afterward the pleasant feeling passed, and he felt the ground and the cold flowing into him. For a moment he tried to curl up his legs as he was used to, but even that simple movement was beyond his power. Sleep took possession of him. Before long sleighbells rang in his ears. He did not believe what he was hearing. His rescue was simple, unceremonious. A peasant got off his sleigh and shouted in his ears: "Get up, man, get up."

"I'm getting up," he answered, though he knew he had not the power to stand.

"Do you want help?" The peasant spoke to him the way one speaks to a drunkard.

"Take me," he said, and abandoned his body to the strong arms of the peasant.

The peasant rubbed his face and asked, "What were you doing here?"

Felix did not understand and said, "Take me home. My house isn't far from here."

"Where is your house?" the peasant interrogated him.

"The hotel," he managed to say before falling asleep. But the peasant wouldn't let him sleep. He kneaded his body like dough with both hands. Felix felt his fingers in his cold flesh. Afterward he picked Felix up and put him on the straw in his sleigh. When he woke, it seemed he had set out a short time ago. How had he gone so far? He wanted to ask the driver, but he immediately realized that it had nothing to do with the driver.

The way to the inn was short. "We're here," the peasant announced. Felix took a hundred-crown note from his coat pocket and handed it to him. "That isn't the sum I asked for," the peasant said in a peasant voice. Felix did not bargain with him and doubled the sum. The peasant slowly let him down, stood him on his feet, and led him to the entrance. He immediately mounted his sleigh. Felix was barely aware of the surge of his swift disappearance.

Everyone was already asleep in bed. Only one lamp, a round one, was lit in the dining room.

"You aren't asleep, sir?" asked the servant.

"I've come back from a hike. Could you serve me a cup of coffee?"

"With pleasure, but first I must heat the water."

"I would be very grateful."

"How is it outside?"

"Cold, very cold."

"I thought so. The chimneys are roaring."

In a quarter of an hour the servant woman brought him two pieces of bread spread with butter, a pickled cucumber, and a cup of hot coffee. He was hungry, and the sight of the tray increased his hunger. "Thank you," he repeated.

"Think nothing of it," she answered in German.

"No one was worried about me," the thought passed through his brain. "I might have disappeared." Out loud he inquired, "Didn't they ask about me?"

"No, why? Everyone went to sleep on time."

"Then everything is as it should be?"

"Thank God."

Now he no longer remembered why he had gone out and how he had reached that bright grove. Even the face of the peasant, his rescuer, was forgotten. A kind of oblivion enveloped him. In truth, it was fatigue. It overcame him wordlessly on the narrow sofa.

XI

SNOW FELL UNABATED. Early in the morning the servant women cleared the blocked doorways—a fruitless task. A white sea swelled up on all sides, inundating everything. The tall trees seemed like pitiful stakes, unrooted.

"Permit me to thank you," Felix addressed the innkeeper.

"For what?" He was surprised.

"For saving my daughter, Helga." He tried to speak softly.

The innkeeper looked down.

Once a day Felix entered Helga's room and sat at some distance from her bed. "How are you, Father?" She would speak to him as she had never spoken to him in the past.

91

"I am fine, excellent," he exaggerated.

Her face did not open. Each day a new spot would appear on her skin. Her large, lovely eyes, which he loved to look at, sank ever deeper in their sockets. Her flowing, honey-colored hair grew thin and dry. In fact, the bad symptoms did not pain him, but rather the way she addressed him. She conversed naturally with Henrietta, informally, sometimes as though to a housemaid. "She speaks to me as though I weren't her father," envy said in his throat.

Henrietta was so preoccupied with caring for Helga that she completely lost sight of Felix's existence. As far as she was concerned it was as though he had already gone on his way.

In fact, recently he had withdrawn to sit in the foyer. Stella had emerged from her oblivion, wearing her familiar winter coat. For years he had not thought of her. She was buried in one of the cells of his heart. Occasionally her silhouette would flit before him like the touch of a dream, then disappear.

Stella had worked in their house for nearly two years. At first her presence had made no impression. Thin, short, and obedient, she had grown up in a house with many children, as one could see in her diligence. Her hands never knew a moment of repose. In the evening, after washing the dishes, she would disappear. In time they noticed: she loved to read. After two months of hard work and gaining their confidence, Stella took courage and told about herself: she had run away from home. Her father in the village had abused her.

At that time Helga had been thirteen, and Karl, ten. Henrietta was so immersed in the children's lives that nothing around her, including her husband, impinged on her thoughts. Only Stella, who was diligent and orderly, won her affection. In the course of time they became friends. When Felix came home from work at night he would sometimes find them sitting at the table, conversing. Even then some estrangement had wormed its way between him and Henrietta. Not yet a hostile estrangement, only a wall. He had tried to knock it down several times, merely to encounter another wall— Henrietta's eyes. The children filled her life, he would argue in her favor. He sank deeper and deeper into his business. More and more frequently he would come home late. After two years of work Stella suddenly announced she was about to become engaged. Her fiancé had ordered her to leave her work at once.

"How long have you known him?" Henrietta asked, like an elder sister.

"Two weeks."

"And you're certain?"

"Very."

That, as they say, was Stella's other face: the villager within her, her sensuality. The groom, the son of peasants who had migrated to the city, dressed in the latest fashions and spoke in the slang used by all the men who worked in the small suburban factories. He was well built and handsome looking.

"Where will you live?"

"I don't know."

Felix heard of the matter by chance. He was angry. "Again we'll go without a maid for a month. You'll have to start looking again."

"One more month, till we find a replacement," Henrietta requested.

"I mustn't break my promise. My fiancé won't let me," Stella apologized.

Henrietta, of course, was angry, but when they parted she was not tightfisted. She provided Stella with a full wardrobe. Felix also added to her salary. The fiancé came to get her in the evening. They were a handsome couple. When the fiancé picked up the two suitcases, Henrietta couldn't hold back her tears.

A week later Felix brought a village woman home, a healthy, religious woman who used to work and grumble in words no one understood. The children did not like her. Winter came early. The house was unprepared, and the memory of Stella faded.

The months passed, and Felix became ever more firmly ensconced in his business. Upon returning at night, his face bespoke nothing but fatigue. "How are the children?" he would ask, almost distractedly, in the morning before leaving for work.

"He's tired. He works hard," Henrietta would say to herself or sometimes to him. Helga was making great strides in her studies. Karl, by contrast, was having trouble. Henrietta would sit and help him with his homework. His last report card had been disgraceful. Felix would ask him about his studies haphazardly, not too often. He was afraid of the bad answers.

One damp autumn evening, while on his way home, he met Stella. She was wearing Henrietta's clothes: a winter coat and a beret. "Where are you coming from?" He was astounded.

Stella stood before him and her silence immediately revealed her situation: she had separated from her husband. Later, in a café, she told him: he used to return home drunk and beat her. Strangely the suffering was not visible on her face. An intense beauty was spread on her brown skin.

From then on he used to meet her occasionally. They used to sit for an hour or two in a café. Those hours between afternoon and evening light would pass in the wink of an eye. She was simple but proved to be not without sensitivity. At the table she did not seem like a housemaid, but rather like a person to whom life had given an expressive face.

Those hours in the café imperceptibly altered and disrupted his life. Till then his life had been one of business meetings, business meals, and prolonged silence at home. Now they were suddenly full of expectation. The meetings weren't set in advance, they happened by chance on street corners, like sudden illuminations. He, who was used to negotiations, ruses, and entreaties, would sit mutely and listen to her. He liked to hear her voice, perhaps because she knew how to take note of details.

How long did those chance meetings last? A year, perhaps less. Jewish women do not know what love is. Henrietta never put her hand on his neck, not even during their first year of marriage, a kind of practicality precluding sensual ecstasy or lightness of feeling. Stella was not ashamed to love. They used to take cruises along the Danube or sit in cafés. She never asked "How?" or "Till when?" like Jewish girls. When the weather was fine, they would take a tram out of the city. Occasionally she would mention Henrietta. She had learned some things from her that a woman needs to know.

Frequently she would surprise him: "Women are frivolous and not to be trusted."

"How is that?"

"Thus the Creator made them."

In time he would come to wonder what she did between their meetings, where she lived. In her company there were no questions, only inebriation and oblivion, completely unthinking.

Sometimes she spoke even more forcibly: "A man should never trust a woman."

"Why?"

"Because they're unfaithful."

"All of them?"

"Most."

Those declarations had a kind of power, though he wasn't sure whether they were her own or her mother's.

Between meetings he would look forward and reflect. What did not occur to his thoughts? Jews don't know how to enjoy life. They pursue gain and their careers, and in the summer they shut themselves up in pensions. They have no sense of beauty. The women are embittered and cold. They kept accounts before everything else. Felix knew he was included among them, but that did not keep him from cutting himself off because of their flaws.

Stella, of course, had her own opinions about the Jews. The Jews were good. They did not get drunk and beat their wives. They offered her plenty of gifts. Too bad she had not been born Jewish. Her life would have been different. She would have studied in a secretarial school. Once she said to him, "Pardon me, the Jews are decent."

"How is that?" He was surprised.

"I don't know."

In time he would think about those chance remarks of hers with overflowing love.

At the end of that autumn, in the street, she announced to him, "Tomorrow I'm going back to the village."

"What happened?"

"My mother's sick."

"Why didn't you tell me?"

"I didn't want to make you unhappy."

Felix was distracted and confused and immediately gave her all the cash in his pockets. They walked a long way together. The lights of the city were reflected in the puddles, kindling yellow flames in them. He wanted to add something, but he had nothing. In the end he removed his woolen muffler and gave it to her. Stella took the scarf and said, "Thank you." Thus they parted.

The next day he returned and stood in the same place and looked in the colorful puddles. "Stupid, why didn't I detain her?" Sadness seared his breast. Within his soul he knew that the love of such women does not last over the years.

He sank deeper and deeper into his business, actually into forgetfulness. Henrietta and the children went to Baden, and he remained behind. The long hours on the balcony, sunk in the fluff of the evening, would make him forget everything. Very late, he would stand up and sleepily drag himself to bed.

"You must pluck up courage and travel to her village," a voice would occasionally whisper to him. But he put off the trip from day to day. Meanwhile, Henrietta returned from Baden, bringing with her much gaiety. The season was splendid, the children had regained their health. Strangely, it was that gaiety which brought melancholy down upon him.

Finally he did go. It was a small village, planted among the mountains, far from the main thoroughfare and the railroad. They showed him the house immediately, topped with a thatched roof, and nearby a neglected garden plot.

The moment the door opened, he realized he had come too late. The mother had passed away, and the daughter had once again taken her wayward course. The old father spoke as one speaks of a wanton daughter.

"And where is she?"

"I don't know, and I don't want to know," said the old man, closing the door.

Felix hurried back to the station. Luckily he caught the train at the last moment. The trip lasted three hours. Strange, he thought neither about Stella nor her old father, who had not been pleased to see him. Rather he thought about a small business deal which had not gone through. He was so immersed in that trivial matter that he did not notice when the train reached its final stop.

That summer the children grew, and Felix failed to notice. His world was extremely narrowed. The tramways would take him to and from the office every day. Occasionally Karl would ask him a question. Felix would be surprised for a moment, answer hastily, and return to his armchair. Only in time, and incidentally, did he find out that Karl was far behind in his studies. He met one of his tutors in the hall and was astounded: "What's going on? Why?"

Henrietta was embarrassed and said, "You're so busy. I didn't want to upset you."

"I must know." He was angry.

Henrietta lowered her head and covered her mouth with her hand.

In contrast Helga blossomed at the piano. One evening his ear caught, as though from a distance, spotless tones. It was Helga playing.

In the summer of 1935 Karl and his mother went to Baden. He remained with Helga. Even then it was clear that Karl would not continue at the gymnasium, and another school must be found for him. Henrietta accepted this quietly, as though it were not a question of a permanent flaw but rather a transitory weakness. That made Felix exceedingly furious. Even in his night-mares he had not envisioned a son falling behind in his studies.

The summer was hot and in the evening he would sit on the broad balcony with Helga. She practiced four hours every day, but it turned out that the girl was not only practicing. She was also learning to be observant.

One evening she surprised him: "You always fall asleep in the armchair."

"True. What difference does that make?"

"Why don't you go to Baden and revive yourself?"

"I hate pensions."

"And Mother?"

"Mother is different."

In that way, without his noticing, she intruded upon him. He tried to slip away, to shut himself off, but Helga was wily: "Why don't we go out to a restaurant tonight?" In the restaurant, for the first time he noticed: she was very similar to her mother, even in the way she bent her head. The atmosphere in the restaurant was pleasant, or rather relaxed. For the first time they looked at each other with their eyes wide open, a kind of adoption years too late.

"You'll be a musician, right?"

"I want to," she said. Her mouth tightened as in preparation for an effort.

The summer ended and Felix returned to his business. He would pass his few leisure hours in a café where a table was reserved for him, decorated with an embroidered cloth and a vase of flowers. He would come home late at night, tired and bleary. When Henrietta asked him how his day had been, he would answer, "As usual." His life was emptied of all warmth. He loved no one and no one loved him. His home was not his castle but rather a hotel for the night. Occasionally he would meet Helga. She was pursued by studies from morning till night. The piano teacher tormented her for no reason at all. She would practice till late.

"Why aren't you going to sleep?" he once asked her late at night.

"By now it's hard for me to fall asleep."

"I must remove her from his hands." He gnashed his teeth but did nothing. The notion that his daughter would be a famous musician was prompted by his selfishness, and he was unwilling to give up that small hope.

In the autumn Helga came down with pneumonia. Two physicians examined her and made the identical diagnosis, that it was a mild infection. Two weeks later she rose from her bed. She had become thinner and her face had lengthened, expressing great weakness. Henrietta did not leave her side. Felix would come home early and sit in her room. Overnight a kind of bitterness sprouted on her lips. She did not complain about the piano teacher or any other teacher. She spoke of the need to give herself over completely to Chopin. Felix imagined he was hearing a young nun's voice in hers.

When the teacher, a short, ambitious Jew, came to visit her, he did not sit for more than ten minutes. A kind of restlessness raced about in his eyes, as though the world were about to catch fire, and one must provide oneself with a large quantity of water as quickly as possible. Felix meant to say, "Go easy on the girl. She needs to rest." But seeing the teacher's face, a face gripped by panic, he kept silent.

All that autumn Helga practiced with dissatisfaction and expressions of repugnance. The teacher was content, but Helga was not. Felix noticed: her fingers had lost their softness, the knuckles protruded. It was visible: her movements had become convulsive and cold, her look was empty of any will. She walked on her toes and did everything asked of her with utter obedience.

Now came the dark winter days, the urgent visits of physicians, the overblown, empty words, the trees covered with a thick layer of pure white snow, the hurried departures of the housemaids, the tea served on faded trays without cloths or cake, the silence that would hover in the rooms for hours, Henrietta's questions, heard from a distance, clear and loud, as though she were speaking to a deaf person.

XII

AFTER HELGA'S DISAPPEARANCE Henrietta did not leave her side. She transferred her bed to her daughter's room and slept there with her. For hours they would sit together in the room and read the prayerbook. The words rang alien and cold, as though dipped in a chilly stream.

"How do you feel?" Henrietta asked her every hour.

"Excellent." The answer was not long in coming.

"Perhaps you're hungry?"

"No."

Those questions and answers reminded Felix of distant, closed convents, whose narrow window slits are pounded by the winter winds. There was too little light, and every hour the bells would ring. Once a day he would enter. The two women would fix him with their stares, and he would freeze in place for a moment but do what was nearly impossible: utter a few words. First he meant to ask, "How are you two?" or, "How are you, Helga?" But he would not, saying rather, "It's stifling in the room."

"Stifling?"

"Extremely stuffy."

"What can I do? Can I open a window and give the girl a chill?" Thus she put a stop to the conversation. Felix withdrew, his whole being repressed anger, and he went down to the dining room and ordered a cup of coffee.

Down below he would forget himself for a moment. The servant women would care for him attentively and gently. He regretted not knowing their language. The innkeeper's wife made an effort to speak Yiddish to him with a German accent. Strange, on her lips it did not sound ridiculous. The coffee and cheesecake wiped the pains of the morning from his heart, and for a long while he would sit by the window and watch the snow fall.

For two hours he would sit without moving, and suddenly a mad thought would swell up in him: he would kidnap Helga and flee with her. He was now certain that flight and flight alone would cure her. That thought inspired him with new courage: he would bribe one of the drivers. A driver would do it if he gave him enough. To cure Helga he had to take a chance. The snow would disinfect her thoughts. What she needed was disinfection. He was pleased to have found the right word. That word drew other words after it, and the thought blazed up once again, so fiery it had the power to ignore the gloomy view: thick snow, gray snow streaming heavily for two days without respite.

Thus it was till evening. In the evening he sat and argued with two merchants who had been marooned there. The two merchants turned out to be brothers and had a wide-ranging trade in salt and sugar. They were practical men to whose religion a certain toneless practicality also adhered. They rose early, prayed quietly, and immediately sat at the table to eat. At first their meals had been long and slow-paced. Now they hurried, not touching the plentiful food served to them but drinking coffee and smoking heavy, cheap cigarettes.

"What are you worried about?" asked Felix.

"What do you mean? The merchandise, all the merchandise is going down the drain."

He had heard that expression when he was a child. His mother had used it frequently, also his father when he was annoyed. Now he understood: it was a very Jewish expression, apparently.

"Where is the merchandise?" He repeated the word with a slightly foreign accent.

"In storehouses. Why do you ask?"

"I see that you're worried."

"We have good reasons to be worried. The storehouses are wide open, exposed to every wind that blows."

Most of the day they would stand near the window

and observe the falling snow. They were unable to halt the white flow pouring out from on high as though from chimneys.

"They are considered religious men, yet their only concern is for their money," the thought passed through Felix's brain. If he knew their language, he would be more precise and look deeper. He had a strong desire to express his thoughts clearly. It was hard for him to express himself in that garbled language. Besides, everything he said was merely a tangle of words with sediments of anger. The brothers did not stand idly by. They answered him at length, with gestures of face and hands, condemning the Jews of Vienna who denied their ancestors. It was good he did not understand all their arguments. If he had understood, he would have been even more indignant. Nevertheless he kept harrying them: "Why all this worry? You're mourning for sacks of salt and sugar as though they were human beings."

They apparently understood that sharp reproach immediately. They stood up, and with gestures they explained to him that their entire fortune was in the balance, they had families, and if the snow continued everything would go down the drain. Those merchants reminded him, for some reason, of his father. There was no external resemblance. His father had no longer been religious. He only went to synagogue with his wife on the High Holy Days, but that worry and dread had accompanied all his actions. He too had stood by the window on winter days, smoking cigarette after cigarette. Nor had his business risen to great heights. He died at the age of fifty-six, a hasty death.

His mother had lived a long life, writing complaining letters because he did not visit her more often. True, he did not visit often, but he sent her an allowance every month. She too was now in the World of Truth. Strange, even now Felix was unwilling to forgive his father for not making it possible for him to study at the university. If he had studied at the university, his fate would have been different.

Felix knew his father would have been unable to bear the expense except by withdrawing his meager savings from the account. His father was fearful. His mother did not intervene. He was angrier at his father. His mother was a quiet, submissive woman, and she had complained only in her old age.

Meanwhile, Helga had left her bed and come down to the dining room. Helga's appearance roused the irritable merchants. They forgot their misfortune for a moment and rose to their feet. Helga's face, next to her mother, expressed utter calm.

"How are you?" Felix walked up to her. Henrietta made a kind of strange grimace, as though to protect her.

"Excellent," Helga said out loud.

"In that case, let us go eat." He addressed the two of them in an old, homey tone.

"Just a moment," said Henrietta, taking Helga's arm. Felix remained where he was and let them pass.

Dinner was served festively as though the snow had

not hemmed the house in. Recently they had increased the heat; the hearth thundered day and night, spreading pleasant warmth. "We have more than enough," the innkeeper's wife announced, intending to calm her guests, and succeeding. But not with Felix. He stuck to his guns: "I'm leaving soon."

"How can you go now?" the innkeeper's wife asked in surprise.

"If one wishes, anything is possible."

Henrietta had already heard that defiant statement several times. She lowered her face, which had gotten thinner, but which was swollen with several pockets of bitterness. "If you wish to go down, I won't hold you back. But don't panic the girl."

As if to say "I don't live by your dictates," Felix raised his head, but without uttering a word.

After the meal Felix sat with the merchants and tried to pry information and wily tricks out of them. It emerged that they had been trapped there more than once, and more than once they had dared go out in a storm. However, this storm was unlike its predecessors, it apparently came from the north, from Siberia. Felix's curiosity roused them from their misery. They sat and told him about the region which they and their ancestors had crisscrossed from one end to the other. Now that they were being cordial with him, he understood more. When he did not understand, he asked. As they conversed, one of the brothers let out a sigh, like a mourner who has momentarily forgotten his bereavement.

"What shall we do?" Felix asked him with a very Jewish gesture.

"For the moment, there's nothing to do. We have to wait," answered the merchants as one man. "No peasant would run the risk, even if you offered him a mountain of money." The innkeeper joined the discussion and affirmed mutely that truly no peasant would run the risk in that season. For a moment the men were visibly linked by fate: their imprisonment.

Karl's face had become corrupted beyond recognition during the past weeks, and his entire being was immersed in fantasies. The servant girls were fond of him, and he spent the night with them in their side rooms, hidden from view. "Where's Karl?" Henrietta would ask every now and then. When he appeared, his face was all jumbled up, and meaningless phrases spilled from his lips. When Felix found fault with him, he smiled idiotically.

Felix sat by his side and explained to him that as soon as the storm subsided, they would set out. It was hard to know from his face whether or not he was pleased.

"You must be vigilant, Karl. The way is long, hard, and dangerous."

"Correct," he answered in absolute distraction.

"You must drink coffee and stay awake."

"I'll drink," he answered obediently like a drunken peasant returning home.

At first Karl's face disgusted him, but now he had become used to it. He spoke slowly to him, as though to an apprentice. As he spoke mercy stirred within him for that overgrown creature who had been dismissed from high school in disgrace and in the vocational school had been reminded that he was Jewish. If he had not stood out on the football team, they would have picked on him. Now he was here. Why had they brought him here? He had to be taken away from here quickly. He would become completely stupid. He needed to study—organized studies. He had already lost a year of school. If they did not leave quickly, he would lose a second year.

XIII

THE DAYS PASSED and the storm did not abate, changing only in tone. Now it was darker and shot through with lumps of ice on the surface of the drifts. The servant women labored day and night to clear the snow. There was no end to that vain labor. Felix would sit for most of the day in the dining room, drinking coffee and smoking cigarettes. Once a day he would enter Helga's room.

"You haven't left yet?" Helga surprised him.

"No, dear." He restrained his voice as much as he could. "The storm is raging. Wouldn't you like to come with me?"

"No, Father. Today I started reading the Bible with Mother. That's important, isn't it?"

"You won't play anymore?"

111

"I'll play, but not now. Now I need to study the Bible."

"And what shall I tell the teacher?"

"Give him my greetings." The words left her mouth as cold as ice.

"I'm no longer needed by her. She's in her mother's clutches, and that ancient ghost language's. I'm no longer necessary to her." A chill went down his back.

Henrietta sat at her side without intervening. Now her face was like a nurse's. Her eyes were alert and poised to serve her daughter—a submissive servant.

"Won't Helga play anymore?" he asked, turning to Henrietta.

"Why do you ask me?" Henrietta was startled.

"I won't ask. But how much time do you intend to stay here?"

"I'll ask the healer."

"You live by his dictates, I see."

Helga followed that exchange with tense heedfulness. She did not intervene.

Henrietta raised her hand strangely and said, "Who helped us more? Doctors?"

"If that's how things are, take her to a convent." Felix spoke rudely.

"We're Jewish." Henrietta spoke in a soft, irritating voice. "We won't worship idols."

"Idols?" Felix wanted to correct that grave error.

"What should we say, then?"

"Why are you asking me?"

Felix knew that Helga was not under his jurisdiction. She was her mother's prisoner, but it still angered him

112

that his beloved daughter had asked him, "Haven't you left yet?" "If that's what she wants, I'll go. If there's no choice, I'll go."

He sat with the merchants for hours, playing chess. They were good players and it demanded a great effort from him to respond to their sophisticated moves. Now they were more relaxed and returned to their moderate way of life: rising early, praying, and sitting at the table for a long time. Their worries had faded, as though they had realized that a person must not challenge the Lord's explicit will. Their practical faces had not changed at all. On the contrary, now that they were reconciled to the situation, a kind of tranquility impregnated their faces. They ate with a hearty appetite, and in the afternoon they went up to their rooms and slept.

Felix sat with the servant woman who had worked for Jews and spoke with her about one thing and another. Her name was Rokha. She was about fifty and had worked in many Jewish homes: assimilated Jews, those who had converted, and those who had forgotten they were Jewish. "The Jews are a strange nation, are they not?"

"In what way?" Felix interrogated her carefully.

"If only I knew."

"Are they bad?"

"No. Not at all. They were good to me, even when I didn't behave properly. All my clothes come from the Jews. They gave them to me for free."

"So what's strange about them?"

"They're Jews!" She chuckled out loud.

Felix stopped interrogating her about the Jews. He asked her why she had come back. Rokha was not afraid of wasting words and spoke at length. She had worked in the city for many years. Her parents hadn't believed she would come back, but she surprised them by returning. A person must return to his home and faith, otherwise he lives his whole life as a nomad. The city is good for young people. But in the end youth withers. What can a person do without her own home? If a person has her own home, a husband and children of her own, she leaves the world silently, people accompany her to her resting place, and she lies there with no one knocking at her grave.

"And now you're content?"

"I'm working. Thank God I have the strength to work. The children don't have to support me. My late husband left me a nice inheritance—four children."

The longer he sat and spoke with her, the more the contempt was wiped from his face. He was trapped in her voice for a moment.

However, he tormented Karl at every opportunity. "You've lost this school year. You're not reading the books we brought. Why did we bring books? You're not improving your handwriting. Your vocabulary is frightfully thin." Felix knew those were pointless words. The lad was enthralled by the servant women, and nothing would help except separation, utter separation.

"The first chance we get, we'll go down," Felix surprised him.

"I'm ready," Karl answered mechanically.

In the depths of his heart Felix could not ignore his satisfaction with Karl, who related to the servant girls with absolute freedom. He was not apprehensive or fearful. He had a simple, strong way with women. Women liked him.

While the storm yet raged, a sleigh stopped before the entrance: a Jew had risked his life and gone out. He lightly removed a fur blanket from his knees and with an agile step he approached the door. "Here he is!" Everyone burst into the corridor. "He's come! He's come!" The news passed from mouth to ear till it lodged in the cellar, where the servant women were sorting potatoes.

Thus it was every winter. While no one was expecting a sign of life from the outside world, he would appear and immediately acquire new admirers, particularly female ones. By common consent he was an easygoing man, always inspiring a kind of joy, like a brother. He had a little gift for everyone: a bottle of cologne or an embroidered handkerchief. Not expensive things, but in each was hidden a spark of city splendor. Frequently a servant girl would burst into tears at the sight of a pendant or pin. She remembered: not many years ago she had been in the city, strolling through the streets, and on Sundays she would buy a double portion of cherry ice cream. Now she was here, in this desolate place, without friends or lovers.

They immediately scurried about and brought him the best there was: only at the round table was his wiry thinness visible. He was not a splendid-looking person.

His coat was faded, his vest tattered, and his gestures were also without charm. Were it not for his eyes, he would look like one of the plodding merchants who show up here in the spring, sleeping over and setting out without leaving any impression. His eyes sparkled with mischief: once again he had managed to outdo the blind, white giant. He had done it again.

"We always lose out, because we're afraid of taking a risk," the merchant said in a provocative tone.

"Do you want us to behave like madmen?" his brother replied.

"A person who takes no risks always loses out, don't you agree?"

"A Jew doesn't risk his life."

The people surrounded this man and looked at him with admiration. "Weren't you afraid?" "How did you feel?" "What were you thinking about?" Apparently he liked being admired. It seemed as though he had come only in order to be admired for a moment. The proprietors indulged him, plying him with plenty of hot food. The servant women would also get their pleasure. But that open admiration brought a kind of melancholy down upon Felix. "Haven't you gone yet?" his beloved daughter had asked him. It was hard to uproot that sentence from his heart.

In the evening he sat with the guest. It turned out he was not a merchant but employed in the service of the merchants, transferring money or merchandise for a percentage. That permitted him to rest during the summer.

"How did you overcome fear?" Felix interrogated him.

"Life is not important to me."

"When did you acquire that feeling?"

"I didn't adopt it or acquire it. It has always been with me."

"Death doesn't frighten you?"

"No."

"Therefore you are a free man."

"Not completely, to my regret."

"I too am about to leave."

"Why are you in a hurry?"

"My business. I left everything behind, not in dependable hands, if one might say so."

"To die for business?"

"And you?"

"I do it as a sport."

He seldom entered Helga's room. Every morning he stood and listened to them chanting the prayers together. He had a powerful desire to burst in and hush those murmurings. Now he was certain that it was madness, Henrietta's madness. How could Helga be saved from her?

When Helga came down in the evening, he approached her and asked, "Don't you want to go back home? This isn't a home. This is an inn for wayfarers. One doesn't dwell here, one merely sojourns for a while."

"Why are you in a hurry, Father? A storm is raging outside."

"When, then, shall we return home? When?"

"After I have studied the Bible with Mother," she answered with a heavy quietness which stopped Felix's mouth all at once.

Having no other ally, he once again fell upon Karl. He explained to him that they must go down soon. "True, we must take the risk. Without taking risks, one achieves nothing in life."

"How shall we do it?" asked Karl, and it was evident he was not thirsting for adventure.

"Don't ask. If a man wishes, he can descend on foot."

"Do you want to go down on foot in a storm like this?"

"A few days ago a man arrived here. Nothing happened to him. There's nothing to be afraid of. If one is afraid, one achieves nothing in life." Felix repeated those clichés with a kind of assertiveness.

XIV

WHILE THE WORLD still seemed like a dark cave with no way out, the snowstorm died down. It happened without warning, suddenly, as though by an order. The darkness melted away, and the army of light invaded and deployed upon the white expanses. The conquest was complete, without leaving a single dark stain. The servant women went outside, gripped with joy. Thus they stood at the annual parade through the village, cheering and in tears.

Felix too went outside. The great light surprised him with its intensity, but he was not happy. He stood apart like a person whose misfortune has been made public. The two merchants hurriedly took out their packs and stood ready. Their practicality, which had been blunted in the dark days, was resurrected.

"You're leaving?" Felix asked.

"What do you think, that we'd wait?" they answered together, rudely.

Fatigue fell upon Felix. The tension of the past weeks had worn him out. He went up to his room. Within minutes his eyes closed. He slept uninterruptedly for many hours, and when he awakened the sky was already twilit in blue and red, a blue flame flickering on the snow.

For a long while he sat on the bed. From Helga's room no sound was heard. Silence flowed from there, pouring out into the dark, narrow corridor. Nor was any sound heard from downstairs. "The servant women are sorting potatoes in the cellar," the thought crossed his mind. He got out of bed. The veranda was lit for the evening. The light made the heavy, strong window frame stand out. The panes were polished, and one could clearly see how flakes of darkness were falling from the tall trees and slowly spreading beside the trunks.

"Don't they serve a cup of coffee here?" he called out.

No one answered.

The warm armchair enveloped his body, and without noticing it, he was gripped by sleep. He dreamed that a servant woman, wearing a revealing dress, served him coffee and cherry pie. Jocularly he proposed that she travel to Vienna with him. She laughed, for Karl too had made her the same offer.

When he woke up, the dining room was already lit, the tables set, and the dream faded from his memory.

What remained in the hollow of his body was the thirst for coffee, and that impelled him to ask, "Don't they serve coffee here?"

"The meal is ready, sir," answered the innkeeper's wife from behind the curtain, in a soft voice. "Let's not give up tonight's delicacies. The coffee will come in due time, won't it?"

"Correct," he said.

Only later, when he saw the two merchants standing near the door, as they had stood in the morning, was he completely awake. From the way they were standing it was clear that the sleigh drivers were defrauding them. They had asked an exorbitant price, so the merchants had decided, no matter what, not to move until an honest driver was found. For a moment he looked at them: was it desperation or determination? If he had had the strength, he would have gone out to them and encouraged them.

Helga came down dressed in a long wool dress. Her face was bright, relaxed, as though she had returned from an evening walk or from an hour of successful playing. "How was your day?" asked Felix in a kind of distraction.

"I sat at the window, Father, and I looked at the snow. I didn't do a thing."

"I fell asleep, I don't know why," he said of his weakness.

A smile spread over her face, as though he had revealed a secret to her. Seeing her smile, Henrietta smiled as well. They sat at the table.

The innkeeper's wife brought a tray full of roasted potatoes and announced, "The butter and cheese are on the way. Help yourselves, ladies and gentlemen."

"And borscht," Helga wondered. "Won't we get any of that red, red pottage?"

"We shall," said the innkeeper's wife in a motherly voice. "We shall not deny anyone that red brew."

Karl buried his face in his plate. Distress darkened his brow. Now it seemed as though he was not eating but that he was more and more infected by his gloom.

"What happened, Karl?" Henrietta asked him softly.

"Nothing."

"Why are you sad, then?"

"Don't you know?"

"If you don't want to go away, you can stay with me." Karl did not answer.

Henrietta repeated her offer: "You can stay with me."

"There's a bright future in store for you here." Felix broke his silence. "But if you wish to stay, I won't prevent you."

Henrietta did not respond. Even before that she had not tried to persuade him. Her love for Karl was greater than ever, but now it was not corporeal, if one might say so. In her soul she knew that he too was lost and needed to be strengthened, to be taught, and to be taken away from the servant women. But Helga's illness filled her completely, and no strength remained for others.

In the meantime the innkeeper's wife surprised her guests and served them plum pie. Seeing that delicacy,

Helga's face brightened. Her illness was forgotten. She spoke freely with the old, flexible variety of words, joking with the innkeeper's wife and with the servants, calling the place the "Grand Hotel." If people in Vienna only knew what was to be had here, they would all make the pilgrimage. Karl too was surprised by that pleasant tone, and the anguish passed from his face. For a full hour they sat, drank coffee, and asked for seconds. Henrietta's ascetic face did not soften, but for a moment the old smile peeped out from her lips.

Felix knew that his life had flowed and reached this alien place, and now it must split in two. He did not know what the coming days would bring. Helga's bright face made him forget the fears of the journey for a moment, and he fell asleep lightly.

XV

THE NEXT DAY the sky was low and clear, and the sun scattered its light across the white expanses. The servant women cleared the snow and sang old folk songs. Felix slept all day long. The singing penetrated his sleep without waking him. In his sleep he was in Vienna, in the warehouse, reprimanding the man in charge who had neglected many matters. He was particularly furious about the broken window that had not been repaired in time.

When he awoke it was already clear that he would not be leaving the next day. The last light was dark blue, showing that the frost that night would be severe. He sat on his bed and listened to the evening noises. The thirst for coffee assailed him again. The thought that downstairs he would receive a cup of coffee and a piece

124

of cheesecake inspired him with the will to act, and he roused himself and stood up.

When he neared the corridor he heard Helga's voice. "Mother, when will we go home?"

"Soon, when you're well."

"I am well."

"Certainly you're well. You must get stronger. Isn't it nice here?"

"I always think about the cats we left at home, the poor things. I miss them."

"They're not poor things, my dear. Gloria is taking care of them. She's feeding them and indulging them. You have nothing to fear."

"I'm frightened."

"Of what?"

"That the dogs will bite them."

"They're inside the house, dear, near the stove. Gloria doesn't put them out."

"Won't we go back home?"

"When you get better. Tomorrow we'll go to the healer and see what he says."

"I don't feel like going to see him."

"It isn't far. The weather is beautiful. The snow is very quiet."

Later the silence returned. Felix stood where he was. Now he knew that Helga's illness was mortal. He slowly went downstairs, and in a whisper he asked for a cup of coffee. The coffee was served without cake. "If I had studied medicine, everything would be different." That sentence, which he repeated so often, came back to him. He was angry that the next day they would be going to the healer again. Helga would have to wait outside with those poverty-stricken people. They would certainly ask her questions, and she would have to answer. "Why are they tormenting that good girl?" His voice was stifled in his throat.

The next morning they all rose early, Felix too. Helga was in a good mood and prepared for the outing with a will. The day was bright like the previous one, and the servant women were clearing the grounds and the paths. The innkeeper's wife was polishing the front windows. A clean, chilly smell hung in the air.

The innkeeper brought the tables close to the windows and said, "Precious sun, let's not miss out on it." He had no children of his own, and a constant pain dwelled within him, hidden away, all year long. Even at that early morning hour a tremor of devotion fluttered over his powerful fingers. "The precious sun, come near."

"Father, why don't you join us?" Helga asked in a full voice.

"Willingly, but where?"

"To the healer, the famous healer."

"Whatever you say." Felix was pleased that his daughter's clear voice had returned.

Before long they were standing outside. The broad lapels of Helga's coat gave her figure a womanly, erect look, as in the past. And her smile—true, there was something twisted in the smile, but still it was the same one as after an hour of successful playing, which always brought, though she was unaware of it, a bit of pride.

For a long time they trudged through the snow.

The farther they walked, the better Helga's mood became. From time to time, though a few strange words emerged, most of the words were her own. Henrietta walked in front with short steps, not interfering in the conversation.

"When are you leaving us?" Helga addressed her father in overtly feminine tones.

"Soon. I'm looking for a trustworthy driver. Not all of them are trustworthy, as you might imagine."

"Won't we see you?"

"I have no choice, my dear. I left everything wide open. Who knows what the evil spirits have done? What should I send you?"

"Me? Nothing."

"Still."

"I have a beloved, but of course it is difficult to send him. He's made of heavy wood."

"I'm willing to try."

"You're an optimist, Father."

"Very much so."

"Have a safe trip. I wish you success in whatever you do," Helga said in an infuriatingly dry voice.

"What's happened?"

"Nothing. Why? Have I made a mistake?"

"No. Helga, my dear, we shall meet frequently. The winter will pass and you shall return to Vienna. I will prepare the house. The house must be made ready. It needs many repairs. We have neglected it." Felix spoke in a loud voice which finally was strangled by his emotions.

Helga ignored his voice and returned to her infuriatingly dry tone, saying, "Don't forget to put the cats back in my room. It's hard for me to bear the thought that they're far from me. Oh Lord almighty, how neglected they are."

"My dear, Gloria is taking care of them. She is in the house all the time, feeding them and giving them water. What else do you need?"

"Pardon me, I don't trust her," she said curtly.

From there to the healer's house the way was not long. The snow surrounded the house, rising to the windows. Thin smoke rose from the chimney. The gate, all patched up, reminded one of old houses; once they throbbed with life, but now only the sighs of abandoned old people remain in them.

"Here we are," Henrietta said, an artificial smile surrounding her face. Helga vigorously shook the snow from her boots. Felix plucked a branch with a strange, unnatural movement and wiped his boots.

"Welcome." The caretaker came out to them. Apparently he had heard their footsteps.

"Here we are again," said Henrietta.

"Welcome," the caretaker repeated his greeting. He was dressed in a faded winter coat, the seams of which had unraveled near the shoulders. He had a blue cap on his head, giving him the look of an old-fashioned itinerant peddler.

"How are you, sir." He addressed Felix as one does rich men.

Felix raised his eyebrows, and with a look conveying a good deal of self-esteem, briefly answered, "Fine."

Henrietta, in contrast, spoke at length about the walk there and the snow, as though they were not consulting a healer but rather shopping.

"Sit down, ladies and gentleman, have a seat," the caretaker said in a homey tone of voice. "There's no rush."

"Where is the rabbi?" asked Felix impatiently.

"He is in his room, praying."

"How long will his prayers last?"

"I don't know."

"If that's the situation, we'll go out and walk around."

"What's the hurry, sir? In the country there's plenty of time." The caretaker permitted himself a hint of irony.

"Correct," Felix replied in the same coin. "What's to be done? We're city folk."

Henrietta sat on the bench. Her thin face expressed discontent. Felix knew: his talk rubbed her the wrong way. She turned sideways, her face to the window, so as not to take part in the conversation. The scarf and beret restored forgotten color and youth to Helga's face. It seemed as though she were memorizing a difficult piece of music. But that was merely appearance. Her legs fidgeted impatiently.

"Let's leave here," he addressed Helga, as if they were in a place unfit for human habitation.

"Father, the healer is praying." Helga spoke loudly for some reason. "In a short time he will finish his prayers."

Henrietta sat on the bench without moving. The

conversation Felix had held first with the caretaker and then with Helga had paralyzed her increasingly. "Don't be coarse," she wanted to lift up her head and tell him.

"How do you like our remote area?" the caretaker said familiarly to Felix.

"Full of interest."

"What do my ears hear? Such a compliment, from a man of the city, I have never heard in my life."

"It would be preferable to come here in the summer. In the summer one could take shelter in the shade of the trees." Felix sought to modify his remark.

"I agree with you completely, sir. The air here is crystal clear. But is the winter here so repugnant?"

"Wearisome."

"A fine word, sir. I have not heard it for a long time." The caretaker smiled broadly. "We, to our regret, have a rather slender vocabulary. The troubles of life do not enrich one's vocabulary, apparently. In my youth I loved to read, especially poetry, Schiller and Heine, but now I am so overburdened that I haven't time to open a book."

"How many years have you been working here, sir?" Felix asked, feigning to be at ease.

"Working, you say, sir? I never considered my duties here in terms of work."

"A mission?"

"That would be a bit exaggerated."

"But what would you say? How shall we define it?" Unknowingly Felix tried to embarrass him.

"I am a caretaker, it's as simple as that."

"A fine concept, if one takes it seriously."

"I have learned to forgo pride and make do with little."

"What do you mean by that? I don't understand."

"To admit, once and for all, that our powers are slender, and we have no alternative but to throw ourselves upon the mercies of the Holy One, blessed be He, the Creator of the Universe."

"I understand," Felix said. "I understand, but wouldn't it be more honest to admit publicly that the secrets are hidden, we do not pretend to understand them?"

"Many people have been saved here, I have to admit it."

"Have you seen it with your own eyes?"

"With my own eyes, if I may testify for myself."

All during that conversation Henrietta's face was sealed. She knew that her husband was not asking his questions ingenuously. He intended to lay the caretaker's shame bare for all to see. Of course he did not succeed. The caretaker had garnered some knowledge at that gate, not only regarding people's faces, but also a few precious treasures of language. Once, as he said, he had read a great deal of poetry. Like everyone else, he too was infected with love of the written word, in German. He had not attained true learning. Most of the Jews and Ruthenians who came to that door were simple and did not help him improve his speech.

In the course of time he had become familiar with assimilated Jews. They often were contemptuous of him, especially the men. Once the sight of their clean-shaven faces, their dress, and their erect posture had abashed him. But the years had taught him that people are only people. Fear affects everyone. It was not great contentment that brought people here. Like the holy man, he too learned to have pity for them.

But anger made Felix overdo things. "Are the healer's cures effective?"

That searing question stung the caretaker's kin, and he answered calmly, "The holy man does not whisper magic spells."

"Then what does he do, if I might know?"

"He treats souls."

"That is an exalted and incomprehensible concept."

"Not for those who fear the Lord."

"I understand." Felix restrained himself.

A knock was heard at the door, and the caretaker straightened his cap with a hurried gesture and turned toward the corridor. But before parting from them, he managed to launch the following words at Felix: "Better to fear the Lord than to fear man." As he spoke a mischievous smile spread on his face, as though he had finally managed to get back at Felix.

Felix removed his hat and put it back on. The last words that the caretaker had tossed into the empty room had set him boiling. He felt like running after him and shouting, "I won't sell my soul for a vain belief," but, as in a dream, his arms and legs were bound.

"Why are you angry?" Henrietta raised her head.

"We had heard a lot about them, and now we see them face-to-face. One must have no mercy on them."

"What are you talking about?"

"About this deception. Isn't that clear?"

Helga did not join the conversation. She followed her parents' gestures intently. Felix felt her eyes fixed on him and tried to ignore them. He did not succeed, their piercing gaze disturbed him, and he rose to his feet, announcing, "I'm going outside."

"You're impatient today, Father." Helga tried to stop him.

"Correct."

"I have the feeling that in a little while he'll call us."

"I don't know what you're talking about."

"Do you consider feelings trivial?" She was not deterred by his anger.

"Yes, if one overuses them."

Felix forgot for a moment that Helga was ill and spoke to her in his usual way. In the past, actually, they had discussed the most serious matters.

XVI

"COME IN," a weak voice was heard. Henrietta rose to her feet, and Helga and Felix immediately rose after her. Felix, caught in his own thoughts, was alarmed and gripped his hat as though it were about to slip off his head. The old man, seeing Henrietta at the door, said, "Come in, my daughter. Why are you standing, sir?" Felix was stunned at being spoken to all of a sudden and sat cautiously on the edge of his seat. His lips were pursed.

"How are you, my child?" the old man addressed Helga directly.

Embarrassed, Helga turned toward her mother, seeking her aid.

"Why don't you answer?" said Henrietta. "You were asked about your health."

"I feel fine," she said out loud.

"Thank God," said the old man, licking his lips.

He had wanted to speak with the women alone. Conversation with city women was easier for him than with the men. The men acted toward him with suspicion and arrogance. The old man remembered Felix from the first meeting and was not pleased to see him. "How are you, sir?" He made an effort to harden his accent a little bit, to make it sound more Germanic.

"Well." Felix spoke curtly.

Henrietta, in contrast, spoke at length of what had happened to her since their previous meeting, especially about learning to pray. The old man closed his eyes, and his face grew somewhat calmer from the effort. In a short while he opened his eyes. Now it seemed as though he were about to interrupt her and ask her a practical question, but he did not do so. Instead he addressed Helga, asking: "Do the holy letters speak to your eyes?"

"They are beautiful," she answered immediately.

"Yes, they are beautiful." He was pleased that the girl noticed their external form. He immediately continued. "The holy letters bring us closer to our home—like a person returning to his home village after years. The smell of the trees and the grass drive foreign parts away from him. We have a great many foreign parts within us, do we not? But we, thank God, have a home. We can return home. Do you understand, my child?"

"Yes," Helga said, though she did not fully grasp his meaning.

"Foreign parts are large, broad, assailing us with sadness. The holy letters are our home. When darkness falls, we simply enter our home. Our home is warm and light, and it has all manner of good things in it." The old man smiled a childish smile.

That flow of words piqued Felix, and he moved his chair closer to the table, asking, "Of what foreign parts are you speaking, sir?"

The old man's pale face tensed all at once, and he answered in a very weak voice, "Of the foreign parts within us."

"That is a weighty matter for discussion, but I have a practical question. Tomorrow I am setting out. What will be with Helga?"

"Do not worry." The old man stiffened his voice. "Excessive worry is of no use to anyone. No harm will befall your daughter." Scarcely had that speech left the old man's mouth than he felt that the warm, merciful words he had stored up all night long were abandoning him. Henceforth he would need hard words. Some sadness, old and familiar, passed over him and burned his skin.

"How do you envisage the continuation of your treatment?" Felix pressed him as one speaks to a doctor whose remedies have brought no cure.

"Why so hasty? I can do nothing when I am pressured."

"I'm a father, isn't that so? It's normal that I should know in whose care I am leaving my daughter."

The old man wanted to give him his due. The words

were in his mouth, but he restrained himself: he felt that the man was speaking to him from his pain, and words would merely fan the flames. Silence stood in the room. Henrietta's face was garbed in coldness. She held Helga's hand. Helga's face was alert but expressionless. For a moment it seemed as though she were about to come to her father's assistance, but her mother's hand, as it were, did not permit her. Her gaze, at any rate, never left her father's face as he struggled in that strange arena.

Meanwhile, the old man covered his face, as though to say, "Let me be, I am old, I can no longer bear this travail. Why did you come to deprive me of rest?" Felix was tense and did not feel his plea. He stood his own ground: "I am not a believer. Were it not for my wife, I would not have come here. It would not have occurred to me to come. Regretfully, my daughter has also been affected by that vain belief."

"What evil have I done?" The old man suddenly spread his arms.

Felix regretted having brought the old man to say such a thing, and he said, "I accuse no one. The fault is all my own, my own weakness. If I had been stronger, I would not have been tempted into taking this journey. I accuse no one."

The old man's face fell. A thin cloud covered his forehead, and his hands, which were lying on the table, trembled. The light in his eyes dimmed. What he had to say suddenly was lost to him. He withdrew deeper into his face, leaving the three others outside him.

"What have you done?" Henrietta opened her eyes.

"I spoke the truth. I did not conceal the truth."

The old man did not respond. Sadness increasingly surrounded his face. For a moment or two it seemed as though he were about to utter a word, but he merely pursed his lips, narrowed his gaze, and remained mute.

"Thank you," Felix said, gripping the back of his chair, bowing, and turning to the door.

"What happened?" the caretaker asked him as if he hadn't heard the events within.

"Nothing. I do not wish to speak about it."

"As you wish, but don't become filled with ire."

That ornate expression brought a sluggish smile to Felix's lips, and he said, "I'm not angry."

"If so, everything has reverted to its proper place."

Felix felt the hint of irony but no longer wished to argue. He wanted to go outside, to the cold air.

The air did not soothe his anger. He saw Henrietta's opaque eyes before him, afflicted eyes that expressed a firm will. Was there no one here who understood the stupidity of the thing, the evil? He spoke as one speaks in a dream.

The weather had changed in the meantime. The sky had darkened and heavy clouds had descended and gripped the treetops. No sign of the glory of the morning remained. All the colors had died as though they had never lived. Gray overran the expanses of snow and spoiled them.

"There's nothing to do, I must go," he said as though

someone were standing behind him and detaining him. "Where does one find a sleigh, a decent driver?" Suddenly everything seemed distant, incomprehensible, complex. While he was muttering to himself the heavens opened and a shower of snow poured down from above. It was soft snow, with thick, winged flakes, landing like fluff without even a rustle.

In the dining room Karl sat, relaxed, in front of a bowl full of salted white pumpkin seeds. His sturdy, expressionless presence was not affable, but Felix was pleased that finally he had found a kindred soul.

"We're going back tomorrow, all right?"

"Do you have a sleigh?" Karl asked with a peasant's voice.

"I'm starting to take care of it." He used the language of a clerk. He did not notice that some of his son's awkwardness of expression had also infected him.

"Coffee," Felix called out loud, as though he were not in a tranquil inn but rather a noisy tavern. The innkeeper's wife immediately came over to him. She bowed slightly as though understanding that the man was in distress. Felix looked down and blushed with shame.

XVII

THE OLD MAN did not, apparently, notice Felix's departure. When he finally addressed the women, his face was pale, his eyes burning, and his breathing short and labored. Henrietta leaned forward, and her whole body expressed attentiveness.

"My child . . ." he said to Helga the way one asks a young girl to bring one a drink of water.

"What?" Helga opened her mouth.

"Do you sometimes suffer from headaches?"

"In the past, sir, when I was studying in the gymnasium, but not now."

"In my youth," said the old man, "I suffered from severe headaches."

"The girl doesn't suffer from headaches," Henrietta intervened.

After a prolonged silence, he spoke about foreign parts again, about the expanse of foreignness surrounding us on every side and destroying everything good. "We constantly retreat before that cruel invader, though we no longer have anywhere left to flee." The old man spoke in a whisper, but Henrietta caught every word. The subject was clear to her as though that language had been hers from time immemorial. He spoke of the urgent need to withdraw into our bright, warm homes. "The outside is a lie. A lie." He closed his eyes.

Silence once again took over the room. As though in spite, Henrietta now remembered the way Felix had stood rudely before the chair, bowing and turning his back. It seemed to her that the old man had become weary because of him. Now he must gather strength again. Helga's eyes froze more and more. The bright green in their whites soured, the pupils dimmed. Henrietta was very frightened of that gaze.

Before long the old man opened his eyes. Seeing the women his face brightened.

"Would you be willing to hear my daughter read, Rabbi?"

"Let's hear." The old man smiled.

Helga read, "How goodly are thy tents," in a loud voice with foreign intonation. Clearly it was not easy for her. When she raised her head, her eyes met her mother's. Henrietta was content, and she wanted her daughter to see her satisfaction.

"She recites 'Hear, O Israel' at night," Henrietta whispered.

141

"A person must return home." The old man narrowed his eyes, and his gaze moved away from them. "Return, children, return. The inheritance of the Lord yearns for you."

Henrietta did not understand these words, but she felt as though she grasped their meaning. Helga was flustered after the examination she had just passed. Her brow was all pale.

"We are remaining here," she announced.

The old man's face did not move. He was immersed in some very distant matter. Henrietta knew now that the old man did not speak like a physician, but rather uttered words between pauses and did not always answer questions. Thus it was this time. He did not respond to her announcement. He handed her a book and said: "This is the Bible."

Henrietta took the book and kissed it. Helga's silent face now narrowed, but her eyes opened wide in astonishment, as though she understood her true situation at long last.

"Where shall we read, sir?" Henrietta broke the silence.

"The Portion of the Week, the Portion of the Week," he repeated. It seemed to Henrietta as though the old man were not offering a charm, but a precious brew which must be imbibed in measured doses.

"What else, sir?" she asked like a new servant.

Now the old man's eyes were completely alert. A kind of pride which she had not noticed before sparkled in his dark eyes. It seemed to her that he was about to pronounce a severe condemnation of the falsehoods of Vienna, its assimilators and apostates. Perhaps he would also say something about her sins. Henrietta took Helga's hand. It shook.

"Should we read every day?" she asked, raising the Bible.

"Yes," he replied. Something angry was in his voice. For years he had been confined to that place, without sleep. He rose slightly, as though he were about to implore them—"Let me sleep. I'm old, I need sleep"— but he overcame his anger and said, "So long as one is close to the holy letters, no harm will come to one." Evidently he said that frequently. The words were spoken with no great piety, but rather in weariness.

Both women rose at once. The old man's expression had changed. The light again illuminated his weak face. "Why are you in a rush?" he was about to say to them. "The matter must be examined in depth. It is beyond us. One must sit and listen. Haste is the father of all sin." That silent appeal left them utterly mute.

"Thank you," said Henrietta. She had not expected an answer.

Suddenly he turned to them and said, "I am old, my child. My feet no longer bear me. Were it not for the caretaker, I would not even reach this table. Perhaps the spring will bring me a cure."

"May God bring you a full recovery."

The old man's face filled with light, as though it were not a woman who had blessed him but a heavenly angel.

Helga took her mother's arm, and they turned to go.

"Where are you living?" the old man asked.

"At Hassia's," Henrietta quickly replied.

"A fine woman. It's good you're staying with her."

The old man's eyes filled with wonder, as though he just now grasped what effort had been necessary for that small woman to overcome so much and come so far, how many constraints and confusions she had. Wonderment increasingly lit up his eyes, but suddenly it seemed to fade, and he asked, "Where is Mordecai?"

"Who?"

"Your husband. He left without saying good-bye, isn't that so?"

"He's in a bad mood." Henrietta could think of no other words.

"You must watch over him. He is very angry with himself."

"We have returned to religion. It's hard for him to accept that return. He isn't used to it." Henrietta spoke the way servant women do when they talk about sin and faith.

"We are all quarried from the same source, and we shall all return there. Do not be angry. Mordecai is a good man."

"Why does he think his name is Mordecai?" the thought crossed Henrietta's mind. It was hard for her to hear praise for her husband now. "Come," she said gruffly to Helga, the way one speaks to a heavy animal which must constantly be supervised. The old man saw them out without another word.

In the corridor Henrietta placed two bills on the bureau, then they headed toward the bright vestibule. The caretaker, who noticed them, said loudly, "Blessings upon you. A full recovery." Henrietta did not respond. She hurried to the gate. She was frightened that he too would ask why Felix was angry.

"Mother," asked Helga, "why are you hurrying?"

"We must be back soon. Night is falling early, and soon it will be completely dark."

Though it was still early, darkness filled every corner. Henrietta was not content with herself. It seemed to her she had made a bad impression on the old man. She wrapped herself in her coat, and, walking vigorously, she headed to the clearing.

"How did I read?" Helga asked.

"You were splendid."

Henrietta noticed that the two lines which creased Helga's neck sideways had thickened and turned red. She wanted to remove the scarf from her head and wrap Helga's bare neck, but seeing that her hands were bare too, she held them and said, "Don't worry. The hardest of all is behind us. Now things will improve and brighten." Helga did not grasp the words, nor did Henrietta, to tell the truth, know what her lips were uttering.

They climbed higher and higher. Since her arrival there Henrietta's father's and mother's faces had come to life with great clarity; they had been in exile in Vienna, and all those years they had yearned to return to their ancestral home. They had no means, and so they remained stuck in a miserable suburb, living on dreams. Those mute yearnings gave them bright faces. When she was young she had not known how to love them. She believed that only gymnasium graduates were enlightened people and worthy of respect. Only in time did she realize what she had lost.

"Mother, why are you hurrying?" Helga interrupted her thoughts.

"The darkness is about to descend upon us, dear." She woke up.

"I wanted to say something to you."

"What, my dear."

"Father is about to go, and I am greatly afraid of that journey."

"Why? He wants to go. He must go." Henrietta struggled to find the right words.

Helga knew that her parents had not been at peace with each other in recent years. She also knew that the separation would be good for both of them, but nevertheless it was hard for her to be reconciled.

"Father must go, but you'll still see him often. He will come back and see you, and you'll go back and see him." Helga noticed that her mother emphasized the word "you."

The snow slid down slowly and heavily. The landscape changed its aspect, shrinking. "The country fills me with a different kind of life." She tried to distract Helga. "I don't know why. Perhaps because my parents lived here. Apparently I missed these places. These mountain peaks aren't foreign to me. Strange, isn't it?" Henrietta confessed to her daughter.

"And you're interested in those mountain peaks?"

"There's nothing here of the enchantments of the city, but there's plenty of the silence we all need. We became weary of the turmoil. Now we need the trees." Henrietta spoke in a strange kind of first-person plural.

"I agree with you very much, Mother." Helga's voice contained not freedom, but obedience. Henrietta was apprehensive about that obedience more than the other alien phenomena that had appeared in her. She wanted to continue talking to her, but having been interrupted, she fell silent.

For some time they trudged through the snow without exchanging a word. Now Henrietta knew that separation was imminent. She had known it when Felix rose from his chair, bowed, and turned to the door. The coat and hat he was wearing spoke of departure. Soon Felix and Karl would stand at the door of the inn, dressed in winter coats, stamping impatiently, Felix smoking cigarette after cigarette, muttering all sorts of strange words that sounded like curses about the sleigh which was delayed.

"Helga," Henrietta said to her, "why are you so quiet?"

"What is there to say?"

"Isn't the evening moving?"

Helga raised her eyes and gripped her collar with her right hand. The collar covered part of her face.

Henrietta told her now at length, in a monotone, how her grandmother, all the time she had lived in Vienna, had refused to eat nonkosher food and lived only on fruits and vegetables. Grandfather found those foods

147

difficult to digest, and occasionally he would sneak into a restaurant and order a meal. Once, grandma had caught him in the act, and reminded him of his sin from time to time. Evidently Henrietta was trying to reveal some oppressive secret to her, which had been kept within her for years. Helga avidly swallowed every detail. The story moved her, though she did not grasp its significance.

Before long they reached the inn. Felix, wearing his old athletic shorts, was packing a suitcase. Two stuffed satchels already stood in the corner.

Seeing the two of them, Felix said, without looking up, "The suitcases are ready for the trip. This vain fear too has come to an end."

Henrietta noticed the expression "vain fear," which he had never used before. His athletic shorts showed his sturdy legs, but his face was thin, his temples were shot through with gray, and for some reason it seemed to her that it was an untimely gray.

"How can I help you?" Henrietta asked.

"Everything is packed. We are ready for the journey. Isn't that so, Karl?"

Karl stood at the side. His face expressed a kind of awkward wonderment.

"Why are you sad?" asked Henrietta.

"He isn't sad. He's tired. He needs to sleep." Felix came to his assistance.

They ate dinner at separate tables. Felix sat with Karl near the sealed window and told him, with feigned gaiety, that the next day he would go out looking for an honest peasant to take them down to the station. Karl's face was unaltered. He seemed depressed and sad. Felix spoke persuasively to him. "The city, when all's said and done, offers a wide variety of entertainment and culture. Vienna is a capital, but if you wish to stay here, I won't prevent you."

"I want to."

"What?"

"Stay here."

"You're liable to regret it. Believe me, you'll get tired of the servant girls. What will you do, lie around in the tavern, go to the rabbi with your mother?"

Karl was stunned at being so exposed and lowered his gaze to the table. He had not imagined that his father was so well versed in his secrets.

"And what will I do at home?"

"There's a new movie house in our neighborhood, a rather nice cinema."

"And won't you force me to study?"

"I won't coerce you, I promise."

A smile of relief spread on Karl's face. He was so content that all that evening the smile never left his face. He even sat with Helga and promised her that as soon as he reached home he would write her a long, detailed letter.

"You won't forget?"

"I promise." He used his father's language.

After dinner Henrietta again asked, "How can I help you?" A kind of chill moved across her face.

"No need. Our gear is all stowed." Felix spoke in military tones.

The innkeeper greeted them in an uncustomarily

loud voice. Helga once again asked Karl to write to her when he got back. Karl, wearied by her entreaties, got angry: "I told you, I promised you."

Felix sat at the side and followed his children's conversation intently. They were different from each other and had never been close. But now they were sitting on a single bench. They resembled each other, not only in their visible features. Felix was surprised by the resemblance.

That night in his bed the day's events spread out before his eyes. He saw his wife's face clearly, and that of the old man, but more than anyone he saw Helga. Her mother's coldness now spread on her face and neck. Her fingers rested limply on her knees as though she were a Christian girl who had run away, fearful of her parents, to a convent.

XVIII

THE SKY WAS DARK and drawn in, and through the front windows one could see the narrow path leading to the dairy, a streak of black mud that had coagulated during the night. In the narrow barn, the door of which was slightly open, stood a lone cow lowing in a long, gloomy wail, as though she realized her chances of living were nil. The day before, the servant women had spoken in thick, contemptuous voices about her dried-up udders.

In the dining room a few merchants lingered at prayer. Their murmurings sounded to Felix like dirges. The plans that had seethed in his brain all night now dissipated in the dreary day. He yearned for a cup of coffee, which was not served to him because morning prayers had been prolonged. Finally he seated himself in the foyer.

When prayers were finished, he was angry at himself for not having the courage to rise early and rent a sleigh in time. Now once again the trip would be put off. The merchants sat and ate their fill with quiet pleasure. Felix followed their gestures. They dunked the black bread in cream like people who know how to derive pleasure from fresh food.

They were religious men.

Certainly they were religious. They had not a single drop of melancholy.

Then why was he angry at them?

That fluttering conversation with himself, the cigarette smoke, somewhat calmed the tension of the night. He rose to his feet, ready to go out looking for a driver.

"Where are you from, sir?" one of the merchants addressed him in German.

"Vienna."

"What is a man from the capital doing here in the provinces at this season, if I may ask?"

"A personal matter," he said opaquely, without explanation. "Perhaps you are going back to the railroad station? I need a sleigh to the station."

"No, to my regret, we are advancing northward to sell sugar and salt in the villages."

"You do it together? Are you partners?"

"We're brothers. Can't you see that we're brothers?"

"I'm an only son," he told the man for some reason.

"That's a precarious predicament. How can you bear it?" The man was like all the brothers—ten, it turned out—healthy-looking men, sturdy fellows with a lust for life.

Felix's gaze never left them. It was as though they were not members of the same race, but marvelous creatures who knew how to suck juices in quantities, how to chew curative fibers, to gnaw the black crust. Later too, when they brought their packs out into the corridor, watered the horses, and harnessed them to the sleighs, he did not leave them.

The innkeeper would not give in to them easily. He bargained with them, and finally they reached a compromise, paying with coins and bank notes. In a short while they mounted their five sleighs and set out, one after the other.

Henrietta and Helga slept late. When they came downstairs and found him sitting on the veranda, they were somewhat surprised.

"I didn't manage to hire a sleigh. I wasn't quick enough." Felix rose to his feet.

"No matter," Henrietta said distractedly. They immediately sat by the window, without asking Felix whether he had eaten yet.

Felix sat idly on the veranda, looking at his wife and daughter, who had once been close to him. For a moment he felt like standing up and going over to them, but they seemed so immersed in their meal and so contented that he gave up the idea right away. Henrietta spoke with the servant women in Ruthenian, and it seemed as though that language offered her some hidden pleasure.

Toward noon he recovered and spoke some measured words to the innkeeper. "The time has come to find a driver."

"We shall find one," replied the innkeeper with determination.

"I've reached the limit of my time." Felix spoke emphatically, leaving no doubt that he intended to go down, no matter what.

"Soon one of them will be here, and I'll speak with him."

"The fare is of no importance. Responsibility and honesty, that's what I'm looking for." For a moment he forgot he was talking about a driver, not a clerk in his factory.

"The drivers in our area, sir, are drivers. They like to drink, and get angry at every trifle. Don't look for what they don't have."

"Aren't there any honest ones?"

"No." The innkeeper did not mince words.

"I don't understand," said Felix, and something of his old severity returned to his face.

"They're savages. Is that so hard to understand?" The innkeeper smiled.

"No matter." Felix gave up easily. "I must leave here."

The sky grew lower and lower, darker and darker. Fog crawled along the earth, extending moist arms up to the windows. There was no splendor in that motion, only a muddy feeling. From the distance, from the faraway villages, desperate screams filtered in—animals being beheaded in anger. The wails, mingled with the neighing of thirsty horses, frightened no one in the inn. The servant women polished the ovens. The white sand sent a strong odor to all the rooms.

In the afternoon Henrietta approached him and said, "I wish to say something to you."

"What?"

"I would like to divide the jewels between us. Who knows when we'll see each other again."

"I don't need any jewels. I have more than enough."

"And if you ever need them?"

"I won't need them. My business has prospered up to now, and there's no reason it won't continue."

"Life here is limited, and we can make do with little."

"But if you need to buy a coat, boots, to heat the rooms in the frost, to call a doctor . . ." Felix reverted to his severe voice.

Henrietta did not say another word. She withdrew, the way nuns withdraw when the mother superior reprimands their unsuitable behavior. Her fingers had grown thin in the past months and lengthened, and their joints expressed hardness. It was evident that she was silent, not because she had no response, but because she was commanded to silence by the new laws.

Later in the day the innkeeper announced to Felix that he had found a driver who would take them to the station the day after next. Felix was so pleased that he did not even ask where or when. He ordered a cup of brandy and drank it in one gulp, immediately taking a second one. The drink endowed him with some old desire for action and decisions. Since at that time no

155

one was at his side, he spoke to the servant woman and explained to her that this was the finest season in Vienna. In the winter there were excellent concerts and series of plays. Nor had the cinema been a disappointment in recent years. A person could amuse himself all night long, with a great deal of pleasure, if he were only dressed properly. The cafés were full, a pleasurable, purposeful crowding. A person drank a cup of coffee as though he were drinking a magic draught. The servant woman did not understand a word of his long speech. She undoubtedly listened to her husband the same way when he returned drunk at night and muttered all kinds of garbled, meaningless words.

XIX

THE NEXT DAY Felix was in an exalted mood, joking with the servant women, and he went out several times for a breath of fresh air. He also had considerable success at chess, beating his adversary, an elderly textile merchant, three times running. The merchant was stunned at losing. He raised both his hands and announced, "From now on I won't play anymore."

Afterward Felix put on his boots, his leather coat, and fur hat and went outdoors. The high boots were tight and endowed his legs with new force. He felt like spending his remaining hours there in a house with a hot stove, good coffee, old-fashioned manners, and a soft woman. Sitting for so long with the merchants, and Henrietta's religiosity, had stifled him. He drank cup after cup of liquor, and it restored his faculties of will, his confidence that his distant business had not collapsed, though nevertheless an obscure anguish remained within him.

He walked at the edge of the narrow path, on the snow heavily glazed with frost. From the nearby woods thick silence flowed, pouring down into the empty valleys. Crows hopped from branch to branch, cawing with hunger.

He had no choice but to enter the buffet. At that time a few merchants and passersby were sitting there. The owner's daughter Rosa, a full-figured woman wearing a green shirt, served sandwiches and cakes with both hands. The merchants clearly liked her and her food. Felix sat at the window and watched that earthy activity.

He had been in these mountains for six months. Now it seemed like one long day, leaving only a few dark patches in his consciousness. He tried to console himself that tomorrow's journey would erase them. But the words reminded him, though he did not notice, of Helga's fingers. Since her arrival they had become very thin, not the fingers of a pianist but those of a bank clerk, from which the darkness of the room and rapid writing had wrung all the marrow.

"May I help you, sir?" Rosa addressed Felix with a bright face. "We haven't seen you for a long time, sir. Where were you during the great frost? Did you forget us?" She spoke like a housekeeper whose uniform permits her to speak not only to the servants but also to the masters of the house.

158

"A drink, miss, a drink of refined vodka." Felix spoke in a voice full of craving.

"You mean a little bottle?"

"Why not, if it's refined vodka."

"A little bottle will warm your heart, I'm certain."

That feminine way of speaking to him, warm and devoted, thrilled him. For a moment he felt like rising and kissing her neck, but he refrained; the merchants, with their physicality, cluttered the space.

"Tomorrow I'm going back to Vienna," Felix said, speaking with the thick voice of a peasant.

"Too bad. Why?" she said, showing two silvery teeth that seemed well anchored in her gums.

"Everyone to his own fate, isn't that what they say?"

"Too bad. You brought a breath of the big city to this neglected spot. Provinciality has rotted away our will. Every day the same dismal sight, and now you are leaving us for the luxuries of the city."

"Your German is excellent. Where did you learn it?"

"My father didn't send me to gymnasium. I learned from the old newspapers and magazines that the merchants bring to wrap their wares. Not at gymnasium, sir. I'm embarrassed to admit I've never been to the city."

"No cause for regret."

"I would willingly leave this swamp. But how can one withdraw one's feet? Everything here is muddy." As though to demonstrate, she raised her dress to reveal two sturdy calves, encased in leather boots.

"Here's my card, if you ever get to Vienna."

"What a pleasant surprise," she said, again showing her two silver teeth.

"Why not?" He tried to give his voice a touch of frivolity.

"When I was younger, I tried, several times, to get away, but my father wouldn't permit me. He caught up with me at the railroad station. He's a very honest man, and decent, but for me he's an angel of destruction. That's why I'm here, sir."

"You're marvelous," he said, intending to flatter her.

Felix drank and drank. The more he kept on, the more he felt that the days spent there, in the company of these strangers, had stirred up a new kind of restlessness in him. He remembered Henrietta's brown, tightly buttoned dress. Although he knew that the Jews had no convents, he could not rid his heart of the idea that the next day, as soon as he set out, they would lock the two women behind the heavy gates of a convent.

In the meantime Rosa made a cup of coffee and a sandwich for herself and approached him. "How was it here? Probably wearisome." She was pleased at having located an unusual word.

"Rather interesting. One must look at the details. From the details one learns about everything, isn't that so?" Those words escaped his lips and immediately made a strong impression on Rosa. The vodka, to which he was unused, affected his temples first. Now he felt a kind of lightness in his feet.

Rosa sat at Felix's side and he spoke grandiosely about big cities, about the antiquities and the universities. "My father," he quickly revealed to her, "couldn't afford to send me to the university. If I had studied, I would be treating patients, not leaving them in the hands of wizards. It's a sin to leave someone in the hands of a wizard." Rosa didn't understand a single one of the many words he spoke to her, but she was content that a man from the great city, dressed in a plaid suit, should speak to her as an equal. She drew nearer him, and he could feel her soft body.

"When will those merchants leave?"

"Not so soon." She caught the hint and blushed.

"It's late already. Why don't you kick them out?"

"I'm afraid to. They're regular customers."

Nevertheless he managed, by a ruse, to touch her knee. She smiled and said, "Tomorrow."

"And tonight?"

"I'm engaged, I regret to say."

Felix rose to his feet and paid. The merchants followed him intently with their eyes till he left.

As soon as he left, the golden lights of the evening greeted him. The lights were spread, soft and silent, on the snowbanks. No one was about. Two sleighs standing near the inn were covered with snow, and from a distance they looked like two coffins with white cloth spread over them. Aside from that, nothing. His feet were light. He entered the inn unnoticed. Just then a number of merchants were sitting in the dining room, exchanging views about the weather and nature. They were lumber merchants. In the spring they floated logs down the rivers. They spoke in a hum, the muffled voice of water. The innkeeper's wife served them a basket of russet apples for dessert. In a short while they retired to the long, cheap room where they all slept together.

Felix sat near the window, intently watching the evening change. The golden-red lights got bluer. The flames flickered till they were devoured and became dark stumps. It seemed to him that if he just put out his hand he would be able to feel the fluff of the night which had blossomed freshly above the stumps.

"No one's bringing me a cup of coffee. They've forgotten me," the words burst from his lips but in a voice not his own. The innkeeper's wife, who had heard him, hurried over to him quickly and said, "Here I am, at your service, sir."

"They've forgotten me."

"They haven't forgotten you, sir." She spoke to him in a soft voice, as one speaks to a sick person. "They didn't hear. It didn't register."

"In that case, why don't they serve me a cup of coffee right away."

"I'll serve you immediately, in a jiffy."

Felix apparently felt he had gone too far and said, "Thank you."

The coffee somewhat dispelled his dull heaviness. If they silenced the merchants and turned off the lights, he would close his eyes. The merchants were now quarreling vociferously in the long room. A fateful matter, apparently, which Felix did not entirely grasp. The word "contract" was repeated stubbornly as though everything depended upon it. For a moment it seemed to him that they were not speaking of logs and rafts but about his warehouses, which were emptied of all their contents and now stood open in the cold, ransacked. He had the urge to rise to his feet, burst in, and hush them with a shout: "It is I! I have finally found you. Get out, thieves!"

While he was drowsily dreaming, he heard the inn-keeper's voice: "Why don't you go upstairs, sir. Your bed is made."

"I'm leaving tomorrow, sir, at eight A.M."

"I know, sir. I am the one who hired the sleigh." The tall innkeeper leaned over and spoke in a whisper.

"Is the peasant an honest man?" The words he had used before returned to him.

"Insofar as he is able." The innkeeper attempted a bit of irony.

But Felix, who was bleary and tired, was astonished. "How can I leave with him, then?"

"Don't worry." The innkeeper changed his tone and spoke with him as one speaks to a drunk. "Though the peasant is a peasant, in the end he will bring you to your destination."

"You tell me not to worry. How can I not worry, leaving my sick daughter here?"

"We will watch over her. My wife and I will watch over her," he said, choosing the softest possible words.

"How can you watch over her?" he continued obsti-nately. "She is in the bad hands of wizards and fakers, deceivers. They have no inkling of medicine. Don't you agree with me?"

"Certainly I agree with you. We shall watch over her

vigilantly." Now he spoke the way one talks to overtired children who obstinately insist on some trivial thing.

"Don't you understand my concern?"

"Certainly. It's a legitimate reason for concern. Now rest a little. You need rest." He came over to Felix and gripped his arm.

Felix did not resist, and the two of them slowly paced along the corridor. Felix spoke loudly and grandiloquently about the need for the proper study of medicine. "A person must not deal in healing without a diploma. Wizards and witch doctors must be arrested. Don't you agree with me?"

"Certainly I agree with you, absolutely," said the innkeeper, putting Felix down on his bed. Within seconds he had fallen asleep.

At about eight, Henrietta and Helga descended to the dining room and sat near the sealed window. Dinner was served them, and they ate without asking where Felix was. The meal was tasty, and Helga ate it all and asked for seconds. Afterward they lingered at the table, and Henrietta took advantage of that favorable moment to explain to her that the next day Karl and Felix were returning to Vienna. The way was long, and they would have to wear warm fur coats.

"When are they going back?" Helga asked distractedly.

"Very soon, it seems."

"I am at peace," said Helga.

"There's nothing to worry about," Henrietta immediately added, appalled at Helga's utterance. She was angry at herself for having concealed the truth from her, so when Helga went on to ask how long the trip to Vienna would last and whether they would be returning quickly, Henrietta no longer concealed it from her.

Later, when Helga mentioned the piano, Henrietta was even more absolute: "A person can be whole and enlightened even without a piano."

Helga smiled. Henrietta knew that smile and was frightened of it. At about ten o'clock Henrietta asked the waitress if she had seen Felix. The waitress answered loudly that the gentleman had gone to sleep very early. Though she knew, of course, that Felix had come in drunk, she said nothing of it.

"How is that?" Henrietta spread out her arms as though she had received bad news. In fact she had planned to take her leave from him the night before, mainly to prevent Helga from feeling the rift. Now the plan had gone awry.

Helga sat motionless. From time to time a smile would break out and make her lips tremble. It was hard to know what she was thinking. Henrietta was afraid to ask her. Finally she rose with a kind of optimistic gesture, one which she had adopted when Helga had first become ill, announcing, "Let's go upstairs. It's late. Tomorrow we must rise early."

Hardly had she uttered these words when Karl appeared. He seemed sturdy and casual in his thick coat, a mindless playboy, completely given over to his lusts: darts, bowling, beer from the keg, and buxom wenches.

Now the day was done, and fatigue dulled his face, giving it an obtuse look.

Henrietta's compassion was stirred for her son. Just a few years ago she had hoped he would be, if not among the very best pupils, at least among the good ones at the gymnasium. His decline had been very rapid. First she had blamed the sports instructor, then his gentile friends, rash boys who corrupted him. Felix had not grasped the depth of the crisis. When he realized, it was already too late.

"What can I do for you? What can I give you?" Henrietta went toward him as though he had returned from a long voyage.

"Nothing. I've eaten," he answered, speaking sloppily.

"Nothing . . ." Henrietta let her voice hang in midair. "Will you know how to manage?" The old voice returned to her, concerned. In recent years it had been given over entirely to Helga.

"What is there to know?" He rejected her excessive, tardy concern. Of course he suspected what would follow: "Where will you go to school? A person without a matriculation certificate has no future." He knew those rhetorical flights by heart.

"Will you write to us?" she asked in an artificial voice.

"I'll write."

"I beg you." The artificial voice had not left her.

Helga, who had been listening attentively without uttering a word, rose to her feet with a movement of contained anger, and said, "Why is he going? I don't understand why he's going."

"He must go, my dear. He must," Henrietta answered, to put out the fire.

"But who'll cook his meals?" She tried to sound the warning against a new injustice.

"What do you mean? The housekeeper, Gloria, will take care of his meals, the laundry, cleaning. She will prepare everything for him. He has no future here. What will he do? There's no gymnasium in the whole area, nor any textbooks. Who could teach him mathematics?"

"So the housekeeper will be a mother and sister to him," Helga continued cruelly for some reason.

"No, no, absolutely not." Finally the torrent of pain was released from its prison. Henrietta burst out crying, a controlled weeping that shook her whole body. The full emaciation of her face was revealed. The two wrinkles crossing her neck now looked like two cuts which had just healed.

The children were stunned. They had never seen their mother cry before. Helga knelt at her feet in Christian fashion and implored her, "Forgive me."

"It's nothing, nothing," Henrietta murmured mechanically, trying to stop the swelling torrent.

Karl's blunt face stirred, and he too tried to repent for his insensitivity, immediately promising, "I'll write, Mama. I'll write, I swear."

Helga's eyes suddenly sparkled with life again. She took her mother's arm and turned to the corridor.

The servant woman, who had been observing what was happening all the time, said, "Let me bring the lady a cup of water. She's fainted." She immediately rushed to splash water on her face.

Henrietta revived and kissed Karl's forehead. "Children," she said in her soft, old voice. "Come, let's go upstairs. Tomorrow Karl is setting out on a long trip. He needs complete rest." Her eyes were wide open, and she looked at him with wonderment.

XX

THE NEXT MORNING Felix rose early and walked to the window. A few tangles of darkness still hid beneath the tree trunks, but the light was already spread out upon the snowbanks, bright and new. Something of that strong whiteness penetrated his consciousness and set it trembling. Now he remembered the flood of events which had taken place the day before, one after another, and how he had stood shackled and powerless.

He washed, shaved, put on his plaid wool suit, and went to Karl's room. Karl filled the bed without leaving a corner vacant. "If I could only sleep like that one night, I would be a new man," the thought flashed through his brain. For a moment he observed his son as though he were not his son but rather a creature admirable for being what it was.

"Karl, we are setting out," he called from a distance, to test the reactions of that marvelous creature.

"What?" Karl's reply was not slow in coming.

"You must get dressed. The sleigh will appear in another hour."

"Right away," he answered with a thick voice, like a soldier's.

"Don't put off getting up," Felix said and returned to his room. Now his room was cleared of all his belongings. He looked about him. "Who will remember me in another day?" he said to himself in a language he was not used to and then went downstairs.

Morning prayers had just finished. Some of the merchants were folding their prayer shawls and others were hastily murmuring verses. It was warm in the dining room, the windows sweated, and the fragrance of coffee spread out, fresh and sharp.

"Breakfast is ready," announced a servant woman mechanically, but seeing Felix dressed in his plaid suit she raised her head in surprise and asked him, "Where are you heading?"

"Home. Isn't it time to return home now?" Felix addressed her jocularly.

"We have become used to all of you and like you." The woman spoke clearly.

"My wife and Helga will remain here." Those simple women always fascinated his imagination. He loved to look at them, to sense the sturdiness of their bodies. True, from time to time they would arrive in the capital, but as they say, one must see the fir tree in its home, the woods, and not in a park.

Meanwhile, the merchants had removed their prayer garments and seated themselves at the long tables for a meal.

For a moment he felt like getting up and having an argument with those merchants about the uselessness of their religiosity, but they seemed so relaxed, prepared to welcome their breakfast, that he saw no further reason to frighten them away from their habits.

"The butter is fresh, sir, we churned it this morning."

"Thank you. Thank you very much," he said, feeling the soft contact of the first light.

The merchants ate their fill in tranquility, as though there had never been any disagreement among them. Something of their tranquility also clung to Felix.

At seven o'clock Henrietta and Helga came downstairs and it seemed as though they had awakened only a few minutes earlier. Helga's face was rumpled. An involuntary smile twisted her lips. When Henrietta noticed him she recoiled, as if she had not expected to find him.

"We have come to take our leave of you," she announced in an awkward voice which immediately jarred by its straightforwardness. Felix did not respond.

Helga stood, not taking her eyes off him. "We must part, Father. Why so early in the morning?" Her voice was childish, as though she were asking him to buy her an algebra book in the Papyrus Stationery Shop.

He was shocked by that voice, but to overcome his confusion he rose to his feet and said, "Departure for a short time, my dear, a very short time."

Helga gazed at her mother, who did not deny it.

"When will you come back then?" The childish voice did not leave her, but now it was mingled with a kind of suspicion.

"We've left everything behind: our home, warehouses. Arrangements gobble up your time, from office to office, bureau to bureau. And Karl, let us not forget that a proper framework for his studies must be found. Can we leave him without any framework?" He was piling one thing on another in a rush.

Henrietta knew that tone very well, which more than anything sought to gloss over some wrongdoing or weakness. She kept her silence. It was a difficult moment for her. She yearned for the moment when the sleigh would move off and the parting would be over. When the servant woman approached and asked what to prepare, she said impatiently, "Coffee, just coffee, nothing more."

Helga's face kept changing expression. For a moment it seemed she was prey to despair and trembling, and for a moment a perplexed smile would flit across her face, as though she had realized that the words spoken here openly and out loud were without meaning. Other words were hidden out of sight, and they were the truth, they existed.

Felix felt uncomfortable and lit a cigarette, waiting for Karl to come downstairs. "Where is Karl?" a voice tore itself out of him, and at the same time he warded off the looks that impinged upon him from all sides.

Karl, as though in response to an order, appeared and presented himself.

"Eat, my dear, eat, we're late. The sleigh is already standing outside waiting for us." Felix surrounded him with words. He was relieved to be free of Helga's glances. It was clear to him that she had caught the lie but did not dare give it a name. He rushed to the suitcases, picked them up, and went to the door.

"Good morning, sir." The driver greeted him with a loud, peasantlike voice.

"A blessed morning. We are ready and willing to set out on our way." He addressed him, in his great haste, in somewhat high-flown German.

In the meantime Helga and Henrietta had surrounded Karl and urged him to eat the egg and cheese. Karl pushed the plate aside and said in a gruff voice, "Early in the morning I drink only coffee."

"For my sake," Helga said to him in a strange voice.

"Let him be," said Henrietta, who did not want his last moments with them to be tense. Helga moved aside but her eyes never left him. Karl felt somewhat uneasy and went to the lavatory.

Felix, for some reason, did not avail himself of the driver's assistance. He took the suitcases and packs outside by himself. Now all that remained was to pay the debt to the innkeeper, which is what he did, without looking over the bill or bargaining. The innkeeper extended his long, sturdy arm and said, "It has been a great pleasure. We shall retain fond memories of you and look forward with high hopes for your return to our dwelling in the near future. May God preserve you."

173

Felix was moved, not by his tone, but mainly by the choice of words. The innkeeper's wife looked down without putting out her hand.

The servant women observed the stages of this departure intently. They also wanted permission to say good-bye, secretly hoping he would give them generous tips. Without first saying anything Felix took out a few bills and handed them to the cook: "For all of you."

"May God give you good blessings," she said, bowing slightly.

Henrietta and Helga hugged Karl and pressed him to their hearts. Karl was affected by the turmoil about him and shed a tear, which moved Helga even more. She took his right hand and kissed it a few times.

Felix took advantage of the confusion and mounted the sleigh. Hardly had he done so when the servant women and the groom left the kitchen one by one and stood in a row. Henrietta and Helga held on to Karl's arms until he was standing on the sleigh. Felix wanted to bend his knees and kiss Helga's brow, but the large horses, impatient for the journey, moved and threw him backward. Felix stumbled, but immediately rose and pulled himself erect, waving his hand in farewell.

XXI

NOW THE MOUNTAINS were opened in their full splendor, white and brilliant. The sleigh glided upon the upper crust of the snow without leaving a deep trail. That gliding reminded Felix of a pleasure from past days: wandering in the abandoned fields of snow behind the school, where for the first time he had discovered the peasants' red brick houses with white smoke curling out of the chimneys, the logs and white horses gleaming even whiter in the snow, the scattered basins, the strong women who stood at the door of the steaming dairy, emitting strange noises in the language of the dumb beasts. When he was in the fourth grade a brown dog attacked him and ran after him, and in great fear he had thrown his schoolbag from his shoulders and fled. But the dog was faster than he. It caught him and bit his leg.

For a moment he forgot the many dark days that had wrapped him up in the mountain and tortured him. Once again he was by himself with his memories, which had been hidden away for many years, in that moldy soil which the eye does not care to visit except in moments of grace. In gymnasium he had been one of the better pupils, but not outstanding. There were better than he. Excellence did not come easily to him.

"Karl, aren't you cold?"

"No."

"Isn't it exciting to be going home?"

The fresh air restored to Karl's face that coolness which Felix had noticed during the first days of their stay up on the height. Felix did not yet know that the coolness had actually been acquired among women. They had corrupted his feelings before his arrival at the mountain. He had already been experienced. The servant women had scented his maleness right away.

"I did well to remove him from there. The servant women made him stupid. Vienna is preferable to the damp barn in the farmyard," the thought crossed Felix's mind. Karl sat wrapped up in himself and the heat of his body, cleared of any thought. He was not pleased at sharing that pleasure with anyone, not even with his father. "Leave me alone," his look said.

That grimace, so frequent with him, afflicted Felix with a sudden gloom, as though he understood that all the souls surrounding him in his life now had turned and left him, including the one sitting at his side.

Yet isolation no longer frightened him. Life, which

had become a downslope, frightened him now. First it was Henrietta, closing herself off, the heavy shawl she would wrap about herself in the springtime, when the street spoke of blooming and warmth. The green, bulging shawl would spread coldness mingled with mold. Even then it was evident that something within her, something powerful, sought to take control of her. For two winters in succession she had coughed, a dry cough which afflicted the house with prolonged dread. Helga's turn was not long in coming.

For a long time he tried to flee from himself and cling to the white fields which spread out, broad and silent, but he was too tightly bound to himself, shaken by his thoughts, and all that white splendor, with its varied glories, did not touch him in the end.

He turned to the driver, asking, "Is it a long way to a tavern?"

"There's no Jewish tavern here, only bars."

"That doesn't matter," said Felix. "I eat whatever's available."

"You don't observe the dietary laws?"

"No."

"City Jews like coffee, isn't that right?"

"Yes. How do you know?"

"I've known Jews since my earliest youth. I worked for them and learned their language."

"I understand Yiddish but can't speak it." Felix sought to get the facts straight and avoid misunderstanding.

"It's not a long way to the tavern. In about an hour,

God willing." The driver knew pious Jews and assimilated ones. The gifts he'd received from them over the years hadn't made him feel close to them. From the very first he had always felt repugnance for them, the pious because they called all the gentiles heathen, and the assimilated ones because they were arrogant and regarded every gentile as an ignoramus. He knew, for example, that those added words, "God willing," would not sound pleasant to the city Jew, and he was right.

"You talk like one of the Jews," Felix told him.

"Yiddish is a nice language, isn't it?"

Before an hour had passed they stopped at the entrance of the tavern. It was a simple roadhouse, and inside it the smells of mustard, manure, and vodka clouded together. In the middle of the room stood a long wooden table and two heavy benches.

"What'll you have?" Felix wanted to show the peasant he didn't spurn the food.

"A drink."

"What about you, Karl?"

"A mug of beer."

"Tasty, isn't it?" said the peasant after downing the first glass. "It's been years since I've been here. It's a good thing I happen to be traveling with a city Jew this time, one who doesn't observe kashrut anymore. My passengers are usually religious and very strict. It doesn't bother me. I learned the language and customs from them. In another week it'll be Purim, right? Then come the preparations for Passover. Lots of preparations. When I was a boy I liked to watch those preparations. They took all the pots and pans out and scalded them in boiling water. It's an impressive ceremony, and there was something frightening about it. Later I realized it's only a way of washing them."

"Another," Felix called out to the waiter.

"He doesn't understand German. I'll tell him."

The vodka was raw and sharp, and the sausage was tasteless, but Felix did not put them aside, mainly to show the peasant that he wasn't upset by the food, that if they had to eat, he would eat even the crude sausage of a doubtful roadhouse.

"What do you think of the place?"

"Excellent," answered Felix.

Felix was pleased with himself for managing to overcome his disgust. Something of his damaged pride was strangely restored here. He felt that the peasant food had endowed him with a new will to live. From now on the way would be easier.

To amuse the peasant he spoke some words of Ruthenian he had learned from the servant women. The peasant was pleased and invited him to visit his village. Karl, in contrast, immediately got very drowsy from the thick beer, and Felix wrapped him in two sheepskins. "He's sleeping well, deeply," he said, wanting to show off to the peasant, but the driver was already entirely given over to making the horses gallop. The sleigh glided along without difficulty.

Only now did he feel he was returning home from his exile. The dark foreignness was coming to an end.

Henceforth: the language of cultured people, paved streets, chestnut trees casting their thick shadows on broad sidewalks, the pungent smell of the parks toward evening, the soft light flowing from the street lanterns. One after another these images passed before him, as though he had not been in exile for six months but rather long years. Happiness surrounded him on all sides. "Home. No one can deprive us of what is ours." His heart spoke proudly.

But the vodka had clouded the peasant's spirit. He whipped the horses' backs with an outpouring of fury, and the tall, sturdy horses bolted down the slope as though pursued by dread.

"Why are you beating them so hard?" Felix inquired.

"They're lazy, ruined. Just oats and more oats. There's no such thing as a free lunch. They have a master." The peasant spoke with repressed anger.

Felix, apparently, had not correctly appraised the peasant's fury, for he said, "Spare those beasts," which only made him flare up with rage.

"I don't like it when people tell me what to do."

Felix fell silent. Winds came from the snowy fields and filled the sleigh with cold. There was no escaping its claws. They penetrated every corner and grasped every extremity. His feet were freezing, and the woolen blankets were of no use. Karl woke up and asked, "Where are we? I'm dying of cold."

"We're progressing. Don't worry. We're in a cold pocket, and in a while we'll get out of it," he said loudly to him.

180

The peasant grumbled and cursed the Jews for taking him away from his warm house into the cold every winter. Everything for business. Their lust for money was boundless. "From now on I'll refuse. The winter is meant for sleeping, not travel." For a moment it seemed he was about to stop the sleigh and order them: "Get out. I don't want you anymore." Strangely Felix wasn't frightened. Since Helga had become ill, he no longer feared either drunks or policemen.

At around three o'clock a change took place: the winds died down, the sun descended to the horizon, and the woods on the foothills of the mountain darkened all at once. There was a thrilling kind of beauty in that darkness before absolute darkness. The trees stood in their full nudity, graceful skeletons bending with every breeze.

After about an hour of galloping the peasant's drunkenness passed, and his narrow, angry face thawed. His hands, which had not released the whip, returned to their normal position. He lit a cigarette, and his stormy mood died down.

"All Jews speak Yiddish," he said, surprising Felix.

"Not all of them are religious," Felix answered. "Yiddish isn't a language, it's a patchwork."

The peasant did not fully grasp this idea and said, "I don't understand. Every people has its own language. Why don't the city Jews speak Yiddish? There's nothing to be ashamed of."

"It's not a question of shame."

"But of what?"

"German is higher."

"German is the language of the Germans, right?"

Felix did not answer. The conversation made him ill at ease. It sowed discomfort in him. But that was not the end of it. After a moment of silence, and when it seemed that they were nearing the station, the peasant surprised him again and said, "How did you like our old man?"

"I didn't go to him," he quickly answered.

"Too bad. A holy man. Jews are not the only ones who gather at his doorstep."

"My wife and daughter went to him." Felix did not conceal the truth.

"A holy man. Many people owe him a debt of gratitude. My cousin, a young man, was possessed by a dybbuk, and no one knew what to do. The old man received him and spoke to him. He spoke our language and cured him."

"Completely?"

"Completely, as I live and breathe. He married and has children."

"How did he do it?"

"What do you mean? He drove the dybbuk out. Don't you believe?" When Felix's answer was slow in coming, the peasant came to his assistance. "City Jews are heretics. Too bad they're heretics. God will surely help them one day." He spoke in peasant tones, pious and pompous.

Felix did not trouble to answer him. The darkness was total. They traversed it in silence.

"Karl?" Felix addressed him out loud.

"What, Father?"

"I wanted to know if you were awake. It's getting colder. You mustn't sleep in cold like this."

"I'm not sleeping," he said, and it sounded as if just then he had been aroused from deep slumber.

XXII

THAT EVENING they reached the station. Felix paid the full amount, but the driver was not content, arguing that the journey had been difficult and he deserved extra. Felix did not bargain. The driver put the extra money in his vest pocket and turned the horses around. Felix was glad to be rid of him. Better a bustling station than a hostile driver.

It was a wooden station, and people hung upon its heavy posts like swarming bees. Sacks lay at the side, sacks loaded with grain and salt. Two horses next to the shed neighed thirstily now and then. No one knew anything. A flutter of agitation, remaining after everything was over and done with, haunted the people sprawled there, a kind of ancient fatalism passed from generation to generation.

"Where is the information office?" Felix asked, very foolishly.

One of the station officials explained to him in simple language: "When the train comes, it's there, and when it leaves, it's gone. From now on don't ask any more." Karl smiled as though something he knew had been confirmed. But Felix was displeased. The mob lying along the platform, the dirt, the thick darkness, showed him clearly that here one needed the patience and the tranquility of a beast of the field.

He was weary from all he had undergone in the past few months, tired of himself. The night swooped down, laying its darkness upon the bodies sprawled there. The two hanging lanterns merely intensified the darkness below. "What am I doing here?" Felix wondered, as in a nightmare.

But in the meantime their eyes located another corner. Near the kiosk a few Jews were standing and selling old clothes. Their faces looked serious and pale, as though they were not selling old clothing but rather shaking with fear of heights. They placed the money in their heavy, swollen pockets. They were utterly foreign, utterly different. Menace stared at them from all sides. They tried to charm it away, to make it turn aside—perhaps they could bribe it.

Later a rumor was heard, rousing the people from where they lay—a train was arriving. Lots of children stood at the edge of the platform yelling, "The locomotive!" The rumor proved to be false. It was a small freight train loaded with coal, lazily meandering down the track and passing them. Some of the peasants rose to their feet and roared mighty shouts of abuse at it.

Afterward they lit bonfires and placed chunks of meat and potatoes upon them. The sweet smell of smoking meat rose in the air. The peasants' flushed faces expressed patience and quiet pleasure. Felix stood where he was and observed that simple pleasure with courteous respect. Now he knew that active life could never be recovered. What he had not done by then would never be done. Others would establish great enterprises, would change industry, study at the university. He would no longer do anything. He would perish with his factory in Brundschaugasse. He regretted the pointless passing of his life.

"Father," Karl roused him.

"What is it?"

"Why don't we sit down? Everyone's sitting down. Let's sit down too."

"As you wish. I have no objection," Felix said in a voice not his own.

They sat by one of the fires. The peasants ate and drank, and the more they did, the happier they grew. Felix was so involved with himself that he did not even notice when they offered Karl a hunk of meat and a plate of potatoes. Only after he returned the plate to its owner did Felix realize that Karl had not hesitated to accept. For a moment he felt like reprimanding him, but he immediately smiled, as though he, not his son, had been caught in a deception.

He was still smiling when a peasant approached him and asked for a cigarette in Ruthenian. Felix understood his request and handed him a cigarette. The man bowed and blessed him. His bow, the way he took the cigarette, leaned over, and picked up a twig to light it, those movements, for some reason, reminded Felix of Henrietta's frozen face as she had stood at the door. In vain he searched that face for some sign of sorrow. Her face, in the half-light of the morning, had been opaque. Helga was not dressed properly and trembled with cold.

After midnight Karl woke from a nap and asked, "Hasn't the train come?"

"No, my dear," his father said, trying to soothe him with a warm word.

"I'm hungry. I'll go over and buy a sandwich. Should I buy one for you too?"

"Not for me, just a cup of coffee for me, if there is some," said Felix, handing him a bill. Two short Jews, who had kept on offering used clothes at low prices, now sat on one of the posts, crouched and weary, the suitcases at their side. The will which had previously driven them into the arena had now abandoned them. They had not managed to sell very much. Boys approached them and called them names. They did not respond. They withdrew deeper and deeper into their long coats. From time to time a clump of earth or an animal bone would land on them. They didn't react to that either. That passivity made Felix's blood boil.

Meanwhile Karl returned with a sandwich and a cup of coffee. "Outstanding," said Felix, an expression he seldom used. Karl sank his teeth into the sandwich, not letting up till he had devoured it completely.

"If I ate a sandwich like that, my body would swell up right away," Felix thought. "Aren't you tired?" he asked.

"No. I could eat another sandwich."

"Fine," said Felix, handing him a bill.

For a long while he sat and stared at his son's healthy face. The more he looked, the more he was filled with surprise: his son no longer belonged to him, but rather to himself. The ancient heritage of his forebears would no longer taint him. He would be free. Of course those were common clichés, in his thought, and now, at this crossroads, he sought to apply them to his son.

"We shall arrive soon."

"How do you know, Father?"

"There's a limit to being late, isn't that what we say?"

Felix's head was drawn down lower and lower to the ground. Before long he had fallen asleep where he sat.

His sleep was deep but bright. In his sleep he was with Stella once again. It turned out that Stella knew when his train would arrive and was waiting for him on the platform. He was not surprised, and the two of them went off immediately, as was their habit, to the Mai coffeehouse on Herrengasse. Stella was wearing the long winter coat Henrietta had given her as a present. The collar had been fixed up. Her dress suited her figure. She was pretty, a beauty not overstated.

The coffeehouse was full, but their place in the corner was reserved as always. Her face was lively and fresh, and the appetite for life which he loved so much sparkled in her eyes.

"Sorry I'm so late," he apologized in his usual fashion.

"I understood," said Stella. "I was sure. You're a precise person."

"It was a great adventure." He let some of the truth out.

"You've lost weight. Now you have to recover."

"I didn't shave. I was unable. Excuse my appearance. There was no chance."

Coffee and cake were not slow in coming. The old waitress who recognized him from years ago made no comment, as though there were a question of scandal which must be ignored. But Felix felt a need to apologize to her too. She bent her head, a gray head, which had already seen many reversals in life, knowing that man is as full of weaknesses as a pomegranate is full of seeds.

"Worst of all was the last station," Felix hurriedly explained. "Drunken peasants lay on the floor. No one knew when the train would come. One of the officials added insult to injury by saying in bad German, 'As soon as the train comes, it will be there. You will see it. When it goes away, you'll also see it.' What do you say? Deep philosophy, right?"

Stella laughed, a laugh rich with much joy in life. Felix did not spare her details about the rabble who had spread out over the station and all around it, about the uncertainty which had mingled with the odor of vodka and cigarette smoke. There was no way out except to lie and wait and kill time.

"And you drank? Why didn't you drink?"

"Karl brought me a cup of coffee. A cup of tasteless Ukrainian coffee. Why are you laughing?"

"My father, didn't you know, is of Ukrainian stock. Ruthenian, rather."

"A man with no conscience, I saw him with my own eyes. It was good you ran away from him. How did you pass the time?"

"I worked in a restaurant. There was no other work. I didn't want to work in private homes anymore. The husbands regard your flesh as their own property."

"What did you do then, cook?"

"I washed dishes in a soup kitchen."

Felix apparently had not absorbed Stella's answer. He spoke of the urgent need to get in touch with the correct substances, which the earth offers up in profusion: vegetables, fruits, fibers, peels, sprouts, and aromatic plants—all those good, healthful things. "Because we're Jews, you must know, we have distanced ourselves from all that plenty. Commerce has corrupted our morals and our religion has dried up the mystery. It's good that we're here, beside these healthy people who suck up the marrow of the earth and know what eating and sleeping are, coitus in the daytime and coitus at night. And it's good we're here and have the privilege of seeing, sometimes of putting out our hand and touching, the fruits in season. We are lost. Can't you see it in us, that we're lost?"

"No."

"In that case, let it be known to you that we are

devoid of any content, like a fruit from which all the juice has been squeezed. That's why we're lost. Completely lost."

Hardly had Felix uttered these words when he noticed that Stella's face had grown round and her full breasts seemed to want to spill out. He was seized with desire to touch her breasts.

He had just put out his hand when a dreadful shout cleaved the air: apparently a robbery had been committed, and he awoke. Boys had attacked the two Jews and robbed them of all their money. No one had come to their assistance. They were standing and pleading now: "Help us catch the thieves. They took everything from us. We have children at home. What will we give them?" They were so thin and miserable looking, and the longer they stood there pleading, the more contempt they aroused. Karl was not asleep. He took a long look at those two miserable Jews.

"I would like a cup of coffee," Felix said.

"I'll go get it for you."

"Also a pack of cigarettes."

Karl got up and, stepping lightly, athletically, he turned away. To Felix it seemed he was about to fall upon those two miserable men standing exposed now, without their coats, looking like two circus dwarfs whose masks had been torn from their faces by the violent mob. "Karl," he wanted to call out, "don't touch them," but his voice was choked. Now he knew he was far off. Some pleasure had been denied him at the last minute, but he could not remember when and where.

Fatigue tugged at him as with cords. He opened his eyes so as not to sink into sleep again.

The coffee did warm him. He sat leaning against the post and looked at the peasants. Most of them were awake, chatting and joking, occasionally emitting a sort of wild bellow like tethered animals. Actually they were laughing, fondling the flesh of large women, uttering kinds of guttural words which Felix did not understand.

Only here did he see how much the months on the mountain had changed Karl. His face had lost its city coloring, his shoulders had grown massive, his nostrils had widened, and something peasantlike was stamped on him. Strangely, even his accent had changed. All the unpleasantness Karl had caused him was now forgotten. Now he was proud of his height, of the way he walked, bent over, and slept.

The night passed and no train came. A peasant offered him a glass of spirits and asked, "Where are you from, sir?"

"From Vienna."

"If so, then I might speak a little German. I was in Austria for a year—true, many years ago, for the noncommissioned officers' course. Those were fine times. The camp was near Vienna. The streets are still engraved in my memory. The trams. We were young. There were plenty of girls. Have some sausage to go with the drink. You remind me of good old days."

"When will the train come? Is there a schedule?" Felix asked, not to the point.

"Don't worry. In these parts one can't demand too much of the trains. They go slowly, but in the end they arrive. What business are you in?"

"I manufacture paper."

"I thought Jews only dealt in textiles. Paper too, I see. I didn't know. Is that your son? A handsome lad. He's studying at the gymnasium, right? Mine didn't want to study. I beat them, but in vain."

Felix offered him a cigarette, and the man took it cautiously, as one does with a fine cigarette.

"We're used to this place," the peasant confessed. "A man comes down here, gets drunk, and forgets himself for a moment. A man's got to forget himself, right? Without forgetfulness, there's no hope for revival. What will we do? Sit at home all the time and think, examine our hearts and kidneys? A man comes down here, takes out his little flask, and oblivion descends upon him. Not with his wife, nor with his daughters, nor his brother-in-law, nor his mother-in-law, but with his little bottle. That's fine. Don't look down your nose at that old secret of life. It's a tried and true remedy for many ills."

There was power in that simple, coarse voice, which immediately won Felix's heart. Felix wanted to ask him for details about the fields and orchards, but the peasant's patience came to an end. He found other matters to interest him—men and women whom he knew.

XXIII

TOWARD MORNING, in the last darkness, when no one expected it anymore, a passenger train with a few shiny carriages emerged from the fields cloaked in fog. The peasants surged toward it with great force. For a moment it seemed as though only someone with strength like theirs would make it to the doors. The riot was illusory. Everyone squeezed into the third-class carriages in the rear. No one headed for the first class. Felix and Karl entered at their ease. It was like after a nightmare: once more in a familiar place, next to domestic objects, a language one knows faultlessly, vases and newspapers. The dining car was already fragrant with the good smell of fresh morning coffee, rolls, and butter.

"How was the wait?" the head waitress asked familiarly.

"Simply awful." Felix did not conceal his impression from her. "We waited till we'd given up hope. There was no restaurant or bathroom. People lay like beasts in the field. Where are the police? Where are those responsible for hygiene? Is such neglect conceivable?"

"You're right. A complaint should immediately be lodged with the transportation authorities."

"I intend to do so. It's beyond belief," Felix recovered the voice of former days.

"Certainly," said the head waitress. "Without doubt. However, now permit me to compensate you with a good breakfast."

The warm, orderly place suddenly restored the memory of an old pleasure to Felix: summer vacations with his father and mother. Now there was no trace of them. They were buried in the old Jewish cemetery, in a provincial city where there were no longer any more Jews. For ages he had been meaning to travel there and visit their graves. He put off the trip from year to year. In the past two years the estrangement at home and Helga's illness had aroused hidden yearnings for his father and mother. At one and the same time they had passed away, the father of heart disease; the mother, in her great loneliness, had put an end to her own life. Without his noticing it they had been lost. Some time had passed before he felt their loss within him. He had never spoken about their deaths with either Karl or Helga.

Karl finished eating and headed for the sleeping compartment. Felix did not move from the table, and with every sip of coffee he felt that his former life, not rich with action and laden with errors, was gradually abandoning him, and now the empty space was being filled with a stream of darkness. What would he do in another two days after reaching Vienna? The rooms and furniture which, just a day or two earlier, he had yearned for, suddenly seemed cold and alien to him, with gray sheets covering the sofa and armchairs.

"Did you find the rolls tasty?" asked the waitress in a Viennese accent.

"Very tasty, miss, and the coffee was excellent as well."

She was about thirty-five. The years of service had made the movements of her hands somewhat graceful, but not completely so. A certain heaviness remained. First she had worked at a station buffet. Over the years she had risen in rank and was now the head waitress on the train. A cook and helper were under her orders. She spoke of her rise in rank with absolute seriousness, which made her pursed lips protrude.

The hot, thick coffee slipping down his gullet woke Felix up, and his eyes brightened immediately.

"The winter—isn't it so that the winter brings us sadness?" He searched and came upon that empty cliché.

"I prefer the winter," the waitress answered seriously.

"Interesting."

"Because in the winter not so many Jews travel on this line."

Felix chuckled as though hearing an off-color joke.

"Don't laugh. In recent years they've been filling the

first class till no room is left, and in the summer months you hear their language out loud."

"What's to be done, then?"

"I don't know." Her full face, properly made up, expressed earnestness and malice.

"They should be forbidden to travel first class," Felix play-acted.

"That's my opinion too, but I wouldn't dare express it in public."

"It's a wonderful idea, isn't it?"

The waitress chuckled. Her full face, fleshy from regular meals, now bespoke satisfaction. Finally she had found someone capable of expressing her thoughts in words. In her youth she had worked for Jews. She did not like them. They were too "soft."

"That's just the right word." Felix jumped. "You've caught the main point. The right word at the right time."

The morning light was still dim. The waitress's malicious words amused Felix for a moment. But gloom and fatigue once more tightened around his neck. The train raced lightly across the broad plains. The winter had obliterated every trace of green. The streams and lakes had frozen and turned gray, and even though the carriage was heated, it seemed to him that dampness was about to invade the interior and flood him. In a short time he fell asleep.

At first he still heard clearly the rhythmic clack of the wheels, but slowly those sounds dimmed, and he returned, as though miraculously, to the mountain inn where in the evenings they used to serve fresh cream, and in the mornings the voices of the men praying had filled the dark room with mournful tunes. Helga did not leave her mother's side. Henrietta was wrapped in a yellow woolen kerchief and seemed like a woman preparing herself for a convent. It was not an easy preparation, and every day, together, they advanced a bit further on the way to that distant goal. Now they were sitting and praying. In fact, it was not prayer, but rather preparation for prayer. The effort was great. The entire yoke lay upon Henrietta's narrow shoulders, and with the power of her never-flagging will she pulled Helga along with her.

Helga was very ill. It was hard to discern her illness. In normal times it was not at all apparent, but in the middle of the night, when she awoke from her sleep and they brought her a glass of milk, she would say, "Why are you giving me black milk?" What good would the old man do for her? He was so aged that it was even hard for him to open his eyes. In fact, it wasn't so much an illness as fatigue and a bad state of mind. She needed long, uninterrupted journeys, which would have soaked up the evil smoke that oppressed her temples. The pressure on her temples was her illness. She had to be freed of that oppression, but how could he take her with him? She was tied to her mother by the strongest of shackles. Every day her dependence was greater. Now they were not merely shackles but actually cables. With those cables Henrietta was leading her to the old man, and with those cables she would bring her to the convent.

Felix knew that Jews have no convents, but nevertheless it was hard for him to free himself of the feeling
that they were going to one. Now it was not clear to him
how he had come to descend from the mountain, leaving Helga in her mother's hands. He ought not have
come down and abandoned Helga in the hands of a sick
woman. Because of Karl he had come down. The servant women were laying him waste. Every day he grew
stupider.

That was not quite true. It was not because of Karl
that he had come down, but because of Stella. To go
back to Vienna and sit down and eat dinner with Stella.
Stella's face is flushed from the fresh air, and the fragrance of pines wafts from her winter coat. When she
says, "These rolls are fresh," it is clear that the woman
talking to you has once been close to fields of grain.
Her hands show it. And if she says, "This plum is ripe,"
believe her. She knows about trees, and even though she
has been far away from the trees for years, the fields still
rustle within her. You can hear it in the words she uses,
but more in the way she pronounces them. Every word
shows she is still planted near plentiful waters and
nourished by the cool darkness of the black earth. Now
he will lay his head down and rest a while upon her
breast. It is a soft, broad bosom, erasing the fears of the
night in a single moment.

When he awoke the carriage was already noisy. At
a station hunters had gotten on with their servants.
A cold odor wafted from their thick clothing. They
had a kind of gaiety one hears only in bad dreams,
flushed faces but not congenial. When they took off

their coats the smell of fresh blood rose from their tight clothes.

From then on he was awake, looking out the window, reading the newspaper, knowing that in just nine hours, unless something went wrong, he would be in Vienna. He felt pressure in his chest but he knew it was just a passing pain. He was, despite everything, excited. In the meantime the hunters had taken over the rear benches. The smell of beer spread through the carriage. They drank and shot the breeze in a language Felix knew perfectly, a mixture of street slang with words left over from the gymnasium. The petite bourgeoisie had been trying to imitate the nobility for years, but they were left holding the short end of the stick. The simplicity they once had, if they had it, had long since been lost. He hated that combination of arrogance and coarseness of spirit.

Coffee slowly restored his consciousness. He sat and made a reckoning. It showed clearly that the cash he had left with Henrietta would be sufficient for her needs for a year. The jewels were worth their weight in gold, as they say. If she wanted to sell them, she would have enough money to buy a house. He had received the jewels from his mother a few weeks before her suicide. She had not bought them for their beauty, but as an investment. That present, given him before her death, oppressed him. The thought that his mother had died in solitude, the last Jewish woman in a provincial city, pursued him for many days.

Once he had thought of giving the jewels to Helga,

but in the end he had refrained from doing so. Too much pain was sunk in those diamonds. But now he was content that the jewels were in Henrietta's hands, and that in time of need she could sell them. He wanted to speak of this to Karl, but he immediately realized that Karl was far removed from such matters, and it would be liable to confuse him.

Felix sat without moving. The dim lights of day passed before him and were absorbed by his eyes without leaving a trace. He was alone with himself, his body tired, emptied of thoughts. The waitress approached him and offered him a choice of foods. But he was so bewildered he did not grasp a word. It seemed to him he had been traveling for many days now to take care of some important, complex business that had to be concluded expeditiously.

Henrietta and Helga gradually receded from his inner vision. He saw them slip away, one alongside the other, calm, as though sailing on a long voyage. No worry or haste was evident in their gait. From time to time Henrietta would turn her head with a surprised gaze. In fact, that was a kind of habit from old times which Felix remembered very well. For a long while he sat and followed their calm steps intently till they were out of sight.

"Beer from the keg," he said, finally giving in to the waitress's prodding. He had learned to drink beer when he was still in gymnasium. The need arose with the first flush of masculinity, like cigarettes later on. It was important to him to show he wasn't flabby and pale.

At first the bitter beverage had disgusted him and made him feel dizzy, but in time marriage and Helga's birth taught him to savor everything offered by the yellowish-brown liquid. Sometimes he would find a moment of tranquility in a working-class pub far from prying eyes, sitting at a filthy table with other embittered men. The thick brew would slowly dull the worries and insults. Frequently he would return home clear of everything, like an empty barrel.

In the winter a mug of beer would clarify his mind in quite a frightening fashion. He would see the way one sees through a magnifying glass, including the tiniest details invisible to the naked eye. Sometimes that vision would also make him feel glad in a very secret way. For hours he would sit and stare at a bundle of leaves, opening one after another as though by magic. He liked that light, rather than dimness, better than any other, but sometimes the fumes of the beer would sweep away all his emotions and leave him gloomy and discouraged, a large, clumsy seed drifting in muddy waters with no purpose. In time he learned that a bit of that gloom of his had been inherited by Helga.

In the meantime Karl had awakened from his long sleep and came to sit at the corner table at some distance from his father.

"We're on our way home," Felix greeted him with a somewhat overly festive voice.

"Is that so?"

"We're on our way home. The time has come to go home. Doesn't that make you happy?" Once again Felix kneaded those worn-out words.

Karl was still gripped in thick bonds of sleep, un-clean sleep, the stains of which could be seen on his wrinkled, sweaty face. The servant women had ruined everything good in him. He had to be rehabilitated. That rude word "rehabilitate" had seized him at the time of Helga's illness and stuck in his flesh like a thorn.

The waitress was pleased that, finally, she had a hun-gry lad who was not picky but rather ate everything one served him. She quickly hurried and brought him plates full of cabbage, an omelet, and sausages. Karl sank into these dishes without raising his head till he had devoured everything. Felix noticed: he had the gestures of laboring men.

But meanwhile the beer had done its hidden work. The long months, oppressed by the winter darkness and the mournful melodies of the prayers, were forgot-ten. Powerful desire gripped him from within: to be back in Vienna, to return to the sidewalks which, to-ward evening, soaked up refreshing moisture from the trees, the wine-yellow creepers climbing up to the pointed roofs and, in a moment of grace in the evening light, refined to dull gold.

"The early fall is rich, rich and beautiful," he said to himself. He forgot that it was not autumn now but rather the changeable end of winter, cold winds slicing through the streets like honed blades. Rain and snow falling without pause. The sidewalks slippery, sullied.

"We're on our way home," he said, turning to Karl, but the words made no impression. Remnants of sleep were still scattered across his face. Now that he was satiated, he desired nothing but to return to bed and sleep himself out.

Felix drank mug after mug without getting drunk. Old, coarse songs he had sung in the gymnasium rang in his ears, making him feel very excited. He was so thrilled he did not even notice that the carriage had emptied out in the meantime. Only a single woman, not a young one, sat by the window and stared at the moving landscape with an avid gaze.

For a full hour he sat, picturing broad streets to himself, squares and statues—all the precious charm of Vienna. Of course Vienna could no longer be imagined without Stella now. Her beauty turned inward in the autumn and took him by storm. Now she was twenty-nine. The simplicity she had inherited from her ancestors still was stamped on her face. The years in the city had polished that simplicity and now it glowed in its full grace. There was no need to sail down the Danube. One could sit in a café for hours and enjoy the blue flowers between the double windows.

"As you wish," said Stella.

The beer was excellent. Its taste improved from mug to mug. But his vision was not as clear as it had been. His head was heavy. A few yellow spots scurried before his eyes. His head was heavy, but his mood was still exalted. He rose and, standing straight, he approached the woman sitting by the window and introduced himself: "Felix." The woman was embarrassed, and blushed. She was not used to having strangers address her. She lowered her head, placing her right hand on her temple as though to say: "Let me be by myself. I want to be alone for a while."

"I am returning to Vienna after a long absence. Is that not moving?" Felix spoke to her openly.

The woman regarded him with a full, mute glance and said nothing. In excited tones Felix told how, not many hours ago, he had boarded the train at a crowded, filthy station. Fortunately he had found refuge in this homey carriage, where the food was excellent and the beer was superlative. That was a fine way to return home, was it not? One must return home in gladness, especially when home was Vienna. There were prettier cities than Vienna, but that rare mixture of seriousness and frivolity was to be found there alone. "Am I mistaken?"

The woman's gaze did not leave him. It seemed that the words had touched her, but they did not bring her to speak. Felix went on to talk about his powerful longings for Vienna. Though he was not a native, it was nearly his native city. "If one loves a city, it becomes one's native city in any case. Closeness is important, delicate contact with the trees."

"Are you a religious man?" She opened her mouth when Felix least expected it.

"No. Why do you ask?"

"Pardon me."

"Not religious. Not at all. I have a feeling for music, painting, and theater. In my youth I wanted to study medicine. My parents did not have the wherewithal. Therefore I did not study. But in no way religious."

"Too bad." She compressed everything into two short words.

"Why is that?"

"Because the Church gives life meaning."

Felix was stunned. He had not expected such a response even in a nightmare. He was primed with many words and almost set to utter a number of categorical pronouncements about religious coercion, but he restrained himself, and in a jocular tone he said, "I am Jewish, madam, Jewish by birth."

The woman removed her hat, and with a very self-controlled movement she lowered her head. For a moment it seemed she was about to apologize for that crude invasion of privacy, but she whispered, "I too was a Jew."

Felix withdrew somewhat. His face smiled strangely as though she had not slapped him in the face but rather told him something important.

"You converted?"

"I did."

"What brought you to such a decision?" he whispered.

"What do you mean? Faith. Without faith one doesn't take a step like that," she defended herself.

"Correct," Felix said, astonished and stricken by her words.

"Isn't that clear?"

"I have never been close to religious faith." Felix chose his words carefully.

"Nor was I, until I discovered the Church. The Jews

have long since lost their faith. What remains to them is only a routine maintained by force of habit, but they have no living faith. Am I mistaken?"

"And the Church has it?"

"I, at any rate, found it."

"Strange. It's hard for me to imagine myself kneeling."

"That's precisely the beginning of faith. You must learn self-abnegation."

"I regret to say I'm of the old school. Faith doesn't inspire me."

"Too bad. Sick people who have faith accept bodily pain with patience."

"Are you a nurse, madam?"

"A physician. Can't you see that I'm a physician?" She tried to speak in a different key.

"In my youth I wanted to study medicine, but my parents lacked the wherewithal." He immediately remembered he had already said this.

"Like all the Jewish boys," she could not resist saying.

"Only those of our race are capable of inflicting so much pain. A native Austrian would not have dared to speak that way," the thought crossed his mind. But he was not angry at her. He sat and looked at her face intently, as though she were about to say more. Her pursed lips did not move. The ironic smile changed in character and slowly grew gloomy. "I beg your pardon," he wished to say to her. But she turned her face to the window. For a long time they sat next to each other without exchanging a word, as though they agreed that a person's faith is not a matter for discussion, and on that matter, as on other fateful issues, silence was preferable to words.

"But my wife has become involved with faith." Felix surprised her with this personal revelation.

"How is that?" The doctor turned her head in surprise.

"Our daughter, our daughter Helga, fell ill two and a half years ago. We dragged ourselves from doctor to doctor. There is not a well-known physician in Vienna whose office we did not visit. We even tried one of Professor Jung's assistants. Finally my wife decided that she must return to her home country, the land where her parents were born."

"And she accepted the faith of her ancestors?"

"In the full sense of the word," the cliché dropped from the tip of his tongue.

"Marvelous." The doctor opened her eyes wide.

"A strange marvel." Felix smiled to himself.

The physician apparently sensed his reservations and said, "For what is a physician, sir? A savior? A redeemer? Merely flesh and blood. Without faith in the meaning of life, in its victory, he is merely a fraud, a witch doctor, a sorcerer."

Felix was astonished by the force of that flood. With his own eyes he saw how she had broken through the wall of silence and how those synonyms came to life in her mouth.

"Did she do the right thing?" he asked.

"Bear one thing in mind: one must never give in to

melancholy and despair. Despair, more than anything else, is man's enemy. Despair is heresy. A man must cling to the virtues of the Creator and he is forbidden to despair." Felix no longer doubted that the woman sitting before him was a believer who had attained faith through hard spiritual labor.

"Thank you," he said for some reason.

"Pardon me. I didn't intend to give a sermon."

"Since Helga's illness, our life has not been worth living. My wife and Helga have remained up there on the mountain. I have come down with my son. God knows when we'll meet again," said Felix, feeling tears choking his throat. He went out to the next car, half kitchen and half storeroom, and stood in the corridor. "Good evening," called the waitress in a thick voice full of satisfaction. She was holding a tray of steaming food.

Afterward Felix sat next to his son's bed and spoke to him at strange length about everything they would do at the station and on the way home. He felt a strong need to be with his son, who was groggy from his long sleep.

"You're glad to be going home?"

"Yes. Why not?" Karl answered dutifully.

"The story's over, right?" Felix uttered that bizarre phrase.

XXIV

THE LAST LIGHTS of day dimmed on the horizon and the evening chill showed blue on the leafless trees. They were in a broad plain where a few black stains were scattered across the white fields. The isolated houses, made of red brick, reminded one of a long, warm winter, a winter full of music and uninterrupted reading, fine coffee, and a woman who does not interfere too much. He held no grudge against the physician but he was angry that an educated woman, enlightened and close to other people, should kneel before images and pray to them. He wanted to go back to her and express his thoughts. But the doctor was immersed in reading. From a distance it looked like a medical book, but from close by he discovered it was the *Confessions of Saint Augustine*.

Now the train was coursing faster. In just three more hours, if nothing untoward happened, they would be in Vienna. He walked over to the table, wanting to announce this to Karl. But Karl was so given over to his meal that any word not directly connected to food was superfluous. Yet it was precisely that obtuseness which brought Karl closer to him with a warm, merciful feeling. Now Felix understood clearly that his life, the life which had surrounded himself and his business, had come to an end. He did not know how to love. There was something bad in everything he did. Helga had not wept when he had set out on his way. Now he would have to travel to Fuerstenberg and ask forgiveness of his mother and father. He had not taken the trouble to visit them in recent years.

But he did not forgive Henrietta even now, though he knew the doctors had been a disappointment to her, that their remedies had not helped, and that she was sacrificing her life for Helga's sake.

It was hard for him to forgive her for taking Helga into the darkness with her, the way she had taken her, and most disgraceful of all, the tone, that pious tone, the high shoes, the heavy shawl, that overweening seriousness. In his soul Felix knew that it was a withdrawal she had imposed upon herself, but still it was hard for him to accept that it was completely ingenuous.

The train stopped. Policemen surrounded it on all sides. At first it seemed like a search for a fugitive criminal, but soon it came out that the search was more general. For two straight hours they raked over the second and third classes, and when they reached the first class and examined Felix's documents the policeman called out loud, "Felix Katz, we've got ourselves a Jew."

Felix was insulted by that rude remark and said, "True, a Jew. What's wrong with that?"

"Nothing's wrong, it's just irritating," said the sergeant, speaking like a prison guard.

"What's irritating about it?" he insisted.

"Don't ask unnecessary questions. We don't like nuisances around here."

The doctor, overhearing this exchange, rose to her feet and said, "Leave that man alone." There was authority in her voice as though she were not an anonymous traveler but rather a commander imposing her authority over those under her. They did in fact return the documents, and without asking any more, they left the carriage.

That incident darkened Felix's spirit. The thought that in just two hours he would be in Vienna somewhat softened the insult. "The provinces, all kind of vile vermin swarm there," Felix summed up for himself. To restore the situation to normal he called out in familiar tones, "Karl, we must soon prepare ourselves. The train's slowing down."

"I'm ready," Karl called from his seat.

"The weather's bad. No matter. A coach will take us right home. We'll arrive at eleven." Without his noticing it, the language of past days had returned to him, as well as some of its assurance.

After a while he felt he must go up to the physician and thank her. Something held him back. Finally he overcame it and, in an official-sounding voice, he said, "I wish to thank you."

"What for?"

"You saved me from those bullies."

"Thank the Lord, we are not like beasts."

Now he noticed that two sharp and firm lines crossed her face lengthwise. The volume of the *Confessions of Saint Augustine* lay on the table. Inwardly Felix was pleased he had not been mistaken. He had borrowed the very same edition from the municipal library.

"We are drawing near," she said and rose to her feet. "There's no way to avoid returning to work."

Felix bowed, and without shaking hands they parted.

The rude policemen had upset Karl. Felix explained to him at excessive length that the provinces always swarmed with sinister types, and for that reason it was better to live in the capital, where there were decent cafés, theaters, concert halls.

The train continued to slow down. Darkness mingled with fog crouched on the earth, and from its midst the round roofs of the brick factory thrust upward. That muddy sight was far from splendid, but Felix was excited, seeing them not as ugly warehouses but rather houses long familiar to him. It seemed to him that the miserable streetlights were emitting a kind of closeness for him. Karl stood at his side, dressed in a winter coat, and his entire being bespoke indifference and some contempt for his overly emotional father.

"Here we are!" said Felix when the cars halted.

It was eleven-thirty. Just a few passengers rushed out of the train as though another one awaited them nearby. Some people stood on the platform to greet relatives. When they saw them they burst out in joy. At one time Henrietta used to wait for him too, but in recent years she had ceased.

Felix placed the suitcases on the ground and took off his hat as Viennese German, which he knew to the finest filament, flooded his ear in a warm, pleasant stream.

"Let's stand still for a moment," Felix said, trembling all over.

"What's the matter, Father?"

"I drank too much beer. Apparently it's made me giddy."

People passed them. Two Jews dragged a bulging, heavy suitcase along the ground. They didn't know how to control the heavy, awkward object. From time to time they would stop and look at it angrily as though at a balky beast. Six months earlier all four of them had stood waiting for the train. Henrietta's face had been firm like that of a person who has decided to scale a steep mountain at any cost. It was hard for him to bear that face. Helga was withdrawn and miserable, expressing only utter submission. Now the heavy smell of rosemary was in the air, reminding him of Christian funerals, which used to file by his window, long and stately. Sometimes he could see the face of the deceased, fresh looking and clean shaven.

214

"Where are the coaches?" Felix asked, rousing himself.

"I don't see any coaches here. Maybe we should take the tram." Karl spoke with fatigue, unperturbed.

"There must be. This isn't the first time I'm here. Go see, dear."

The station emptied out. The lonely lights cast long shadows along the platform. "We'll go by foot. I'd do so willingly. The air is fresh, the rain has stopped," he said to himself, though he knew it was a long way and the sidewalks were slippery.

Karl returned with news. "I've found a carriage."

"I knew you would," said Felix, and he was happy that the old arrangements were still in force.

It was an old coach of the kind that had been in use before the trams became common. "Twenty-three Masaryk Street," Felix called out loud. The smell of the upholstery and the horses immediately had their hidden effect. He remembered that in the early summer he and his father and mother used to come here to spend a few days in the big city, or, as his father used to say, "to breathe the air of the heights." Here they would stand not with two suitcases but with many bundles. His mother wore a flowery dress, a sign of urbanity. They did not have a great deal of money, so they had to stay in small, gloomy pensions, and for hours they would walk through the streets or sit in parks. "This is the big city," his father kept saying. "There's something to learn." Now there was no trace of them.

The horses proceeded slowly, and as they advanced

Felix knew that no change had taken place in those familiar streets but rather within him. Indeed, his limbs were breathing, his feet walked, his eyes saw, but from now on he would have to be more awake, to step cautiously, to choose words, and not waste money. They crossed the unpeopled streets. Around the lanterns the sidewalks were gilded with wet light, reminding him of some old, forgotten pleasure. For a moment he forgot the trials of the trip. He curled up and closed his eyes.

He had barely done so when the horses stopped. Karl got out first and in a grating voice he called out, "This is it!" as though they had come to a kiosk in a station. The driver took down the suitcases. Felix gave him a bill without asking for change. The driver bowed deeply. Felix felt like asking him, "Where are you from, sir?" but he immediately realized it was late and that this was certainly his last fare.

"I'll ring," said Karl.

"Ring."

No one answered. "Gloria's sleeping deeply. I doubt whether she'll wake up. Do you have the keys?"

"I do, but they won't help us. She's certainly put the iron bolt across the door," Felix answered practically.

After Karl had pounded on the door with his feet a voice was heard from within: "God, what do they want of me?"

"It's Karl. We're back. You have nothing to be afraid of. Father and I have come back home."

Gloria apparently didn't believe her ears, or she was confused. She called out in a strange voice, "Leave me alone. I haven't done any harm to anyone. Why are you disturbing me? God won't forgive you. There are no Jews here."

"Gloria, my dear. This is Felix speaking. We've just come back from the mountains. Don't be afraid. Open the door for us."

"I don't open doors at night. What do you want? There are no Jews here."

"Gloria." Felix leaned closer to the door. "This is Felix speaking. Don't you recognize my voice? We just came back, Karl and I. You can see us from the window."

"I don't believe anyone."

After a few moments she apparently recovered herself, went to the window, and for a long while she stood without uttering a sound. Finally she opened the window and said, "Have you come back? Where's madam? Where's Helga?"

"They stayed up there. They're coming soon. Don't worry."

His voice apparently convinced her. At any rate she came down cautiously and raised the iron bolt as though she were not meeting the master of the house but rather unbidden guests. "Lord Jesus, so late," Gloria called out in fear.

The corridor was lit. Felix removed his hat and coat with a soft, moderate motion, as if he had not come from a great distance, but rather from work. "Is there any mail?" he asked out of habit.

"I put everything at the side, on the bureau."

"Thank you."

"How is madam?"

"Everything is fine. They won't be long in coming." The words he used to say came back to him.

"Thank God, I was very worried."

In the living room the armchairs stood in their places, the vases; the same in the dining room. A strange smell of alien food stood in the air. Felix walked to the window and opened it. A cold draft penetrated the room. She was about to say, "It's cold. You shouldn't open the window in the middle of the night," but she did not. She was wearing a wool coat, giving her a sturdy look. Now he noticed that in their absence Gloria had hung a picture of Jesus on the wall next to one of John the Baptist.

"What's this?" Felix smiled involuntarily.

"I couldn't leave the house unprotected. I was alone for many months. Bad people knocked on the door every night."

"What did they want?"

"I don't know. Evil people or just bullies."

"And what did you do?"

"What could I do?"

That was Gloria. She had come to their house after Stella. She was completely different, not only in her looks but also in her behavior. Very religious. But that did not stop her from concealing the truth and stealing. Sometimes she would feel remorse and confess, begging forgiveness. "It's hard for me to rid myself of my vices," she would say frequently, pounding her head with both fists. Nor was Henrietta strict with her. Gloria's many weaknesses gave her a strange kind of pleasure. "What can be done?" Henrietta would say with excessive forgiveness.

In the children's rooms the embroidered sheets which Henrietta had placed on the beds were still spread out. He remembered how she had laid them there, one after the other, with a shaking motion, how she had gone and smoothed them carefully afterward.

"No one asked for me?"

"No."

"Good."

Karl did not listen to this conversation. He took off his shoes with a motion habitual with him from childhood, then curled up on the sofa and fell right asleep.

"How is madam? Is she well?"

"Fine. She's become more religious."

"And how is Helga?"

"No change."

"May God send her a full recovery."

Strangely, at that moment he was not moved. The alien odor had left the living room and from close up he noticed what she had changed. Actually not much. Still, in a short time she had stamped her spirit on every object. It was clear to him she had searched through all the drawers, all the shelves in the cupboards, read letters, leafed through family albums, drunk all the liqueurs, and emptied the cellar of all its delicacies.

"Why did you do it?" he asked distractedly.

"What?"

"Why did you go through all the drawers?"

"I had nothing to do. I was alone."

"I understand," said Felix and went to the bedroom. In the bedroom she had changed everything. She had made the twin beds into a single one, spread an eiderdown on the mattress, and covered herself, apparently, with the green woolen blanket which Felix had once brought from Danzig. The smell of perfume and sweat made the room stuffy. The thought crossed his mind that during those months she had not only finished off all the stores in the pantry and basement, sold the silverware, and worn Henrietta's clothes every day, but she had also annexed the bedroom and made it her personal property.

Two awkward pictures hung over the head of the bed. One was Jesus at his mother's bosom and the other was a crucifixion. Drops of blood dripped from his arms. "Take that out of here," he wanted to shout. But he was exhausted. Weariness penetrated every limb of his body. Nevertheless, he gathered his strength and plucked the images from the wall. He opened the window and threw them out into the garden. That act, accomplished with his last strength, prostrated him on the pillows like a corpse, and he immediately sank into sleep.